A Thug Saved My Heart 3

D1568455

By: S.Yvonne

Please feel free to stay connected with me:

Facebook Personal Page:
https://www.facebook.com/shalaine.powell

Facebook Author Page:
https://www.facebook.com/author.syvonne/

Facebook Reading Group:
https://www.facebook.com/groups/506882726157516/?ref=share

Instagram Author Page:
https://instagram.com/authoress_s.yvonne?igshid=191pn9mnx922b

Recap

After I left, I went home first to change out of my work clothes and then drove straight to Cass's house knowing he was there. I decided to park down the street and on the side of the road and take the walk to his house. I didn't even want my shit parked in front of his house to give him the pleasure of trying to clown me. If he didn't want to hear me out that was cool, but at least he could pay me the damn money he owed me for the week. His car was in the driveway along with a few others and Trey as well. I hopped out and knocked hard on the door.

I was met with Trey standing there looking at me crazy. "What you doing here shorty?" He looked like he wasn't pleased to see me. "Cass know you here? You shouldn't be here right now." He frowned. "Leave man, and don't come back."

I peeked over his shoulder and saw straight out to the back where the pool was. There was Cass along with some other niggas including Majestic. Looked like they were having some kind of meeting. "Look I come in peace aiight? I just need to speak with Cass. It'll be real quick." He simply shook his head and moved out the way. "You women are so fuckin' hard headed man I swear. Aiight go ahead."

"Thank you." I replied with attitude.

I went straight to the back and through the sliding door. "Cass, can I talk to you for a minute?" I didn't know what they were talking about but it looked deep. When they saw me they all stopped talking and stared making me feel uncomfortable.

5

"Wussup baby girl?" Cass looked up asking me.

I wanted to fucking spit in his face. "In private." I said. I knew he could see the steam bouncing off of me.

"Go inside, I'll meet in there in a minute. We wrapping it up now." He told me.

I sucked my teeth and made my way inside to sit down. Trey grilled me the entire time. I patiently waited until he adjourned his little meeting. When he sent them all in a different direction to get whatever the hell it was they needed out of his house. "Clear it out." He told them. "We'll be up north for two weeks." He told them and then stared at me. "So what's on your mind pretty girl?" He asked once again taunting me. "Come to your senses yet?"

Now it was my turn to make his ass wait. "Can I use the restroom before we get into this?" I asked.

"Shit, you know where it's at. I'll be here." He let me walk off to the restroom.

When I closed the door and locked it, I put my face over the sink throwing some water on my face before looking at myself real good. I wasn't no weak ass bitch and Cass had me fucked up to the max. I literally had to get myself together to stop from exploding. At the same time, I was losing it because I didn't know what my next move would be. How stupid of me to trust my life in his hands. It took me a minute to get myself together, but right before I got ready to walk out there was a big ass commotion. "Get on the ground! Get on the ground!" Was all I heard.

I swung the door open with my heart beating fast as fuck. "What the hell?" I mumbled. From the upstairs *hallway I could see Cass being laid out on the ground. My heart dropped to my ass when I saw the FEDS up in this bitch. I was stuck. Wasn't no way I was going down with these niggas. I prepared to take off. I rather had taken my chances running rather then walk into that bullshit there. This shit didn't look right. I'm a convicted felon on probation and at this nigga's house. This was a terrible case of wrong place at the wrong time.*

Before I could even get my feet to move a hand was being wrapped around my mouth from the behind. Immediately the tears fell from my eyes out of fear. My breathing got heavy as fuck. "If you wanna make it outta here... shut the fuck up." He growled in my ear. I couldn't make out the voice. All I knew was my life was flashing right before my eyes. The colors of those prison cells appeared so vividly in my mind. It wasn't supposed to go down like this... nah... not like this!

Chapter 1

Leandra 'LeLe' Wells

Those words kept replaying in my mind as the tears continuously fell. It wasn't even fear from somebody grabbing me. The fear was from going back to prison. I'd rather fucking die first than to be living like some caged up animal for some shit I didn't do. I closed my eyes and slowly nodded my head letting the nigga know I understood before he slowly turned me around to face him. The commotion down stairs was getting louder and closer. Now I was staring Trey in the eyes as he gave me a hard look before snatching my arm up and pulling me in one of the guestrooms right across the hall from us. I didn't dare say shit cause he warned me not too but I made sure to be quiet.

Trey led us both into the walk in closet where he removed the rug from the middle of the floor. I didn't know what the fuck was going on cause the tile looked normal. However, in the corner of the tile there was a small latch barely visible to the naked eye. I'm sure that's not some shit anybody would've been able to find unless you knew it was there. Trey quickly removed it and I'll be damn, it exposed a hole in the floor at least big enough for one person to fit; and not comfortably either. "Get in." He ordered with beads of sweat crawling down his forehead. "Come on ma, get the fuck in." He growled giving me a hard push. I didn't know what the fuck was going on but what I did know was the whole fucking house was now swamped with 'the dicks' cause that's exactly what they were.

"What about you Trey?" I whispered as I crawled down into the dark ass hole scared as shit.

"Look ma, don't worry bout me. I'mma be good, they ain't got shit on me."

"I hope I don't suffocate in here." I was breathing fast as fuck on the verge of just passing the hell out at this point.

I could tell he was getting frustrated cause everything was moving so fast and I was so hesitant. "It's designed for this shit, you'll be aiight. Just stay here, don't fuckin' move out this bitch until they gone. You'll know. May be a few hours but you'll be aiight. Leave out the back and jump the gate it'll be dark in a couple hours you should be good." He forcefully pushed my head down and placed the piece back until everything went black again. I could tell he was putting the rug back as well. I really hoped this shit worked.

From a distance I could hear the room door open and Trey being forced to get on the ground. I didn't realize that my ass was pissy until I felt the warm fluid trickling down the inside of my jeans. I couldn't stop shaking and I was worried about Trey's ass. Why would he save me and not him self? This was some bullshit. I didn't know how many hours passed but I knew they were still here because I could hear them rambling throughout the house. Breathing wasn't the problem in this dark ass hole. My legs were cramped and it was hot as fuck. So much so that my wet clothes were starting to cling to my body and I wasn't sure how much longer I could make it down here. God must've truly been on my side because just like Trey said, in a few hours they were gone. My entire body was in pain, but I knew I had to get out of here. I had to find the strength. I slowly pushed the makeshift piece of tile up hoping that I wasn't latched in. I was met with darkness.

Not one piece of light as I crawled my way out met with only a little light shining from the window in the room that barely made it inside of the closet.

I tried to stand up but the pain in my legs caused me to hit the floor in excruciating pain. "Fuck!" I hissed with the tears burning my eyes as I grabbed my knee and tried to rub my legs until the pain subsided just a little. The cold air from the air conditioner had me freezing since my wet clothes clung to my body. I literally had to talk to myself and coach myself to get up. "You ain't no weak ass bitch LeLe, get up!" I growled to myself slowly inhaling and exhaling.

I got myself up and limped toward the stairs and out the back door using only the light shining from outside into the house. I unlocked the sliding door and then made my way out hoping nobody saw me. I almost bust my ass trying to jump his gate but I did it. When I made it to my car down the street, it was right where I left it. I was so terrified to drive that I was shaking again and as soon as I closed and locked the door the overwhelming feelings of what had just happened replayed in my mind causing me to drop my face in the palms of my hands and break down crying.

I couldn't believe what just happened. This shit was like something right out of a movie and I was sure it would be hard for anybody to believe me had I told them this story. This nigga put me in the floor to save me from going back in the joint. I didn't think I could ever repay him for that. It took a while for me to calm myself down and get myself together. Somebody who hadn't been in my predicament before; there was no way they could possibly understand what that shit was like on the other side. Shit was beyond traumatizing. I had worked too hard to try to get my life back. I'm not even healed from the death of Malik, losing our child, and serving time behind all of that.

I remember them cold ass nights in my cells. I remember being thrown in the hole for fighting them bitches off of me. Watching life pass me by while everyone's life continued. Fuck that. I rather them put a bullet in me before they sent me back. It took me a little over thirty minutes before I was able to get it together and pull off. I felt so bad about Trey. Cass on the other hand got what he had coming to him. I didn't give a fuck what happened to his ass for the time being. Trey, however, I wanted to help or at least let somebody close to him know what happened.

The only person that came to mind was CoCo. I know she told me that Trey didn't talk to her but at least if they had living parents or something she could let them know. The more I thought about it, the more fucked up shit was. Like, I realized how much I truly didn't know about Trey. I don't even know if Trey is his real name. I don't have a last name. I don't know where he lives or even if his parents are living. Does him and CoCo share the same mama, just the same daddy, or both? Hell, I truly didn't know. Upon arrival of CoCo's house I could only shake my head when I saw CoCo being led out in cuffs while a bunch of unmarked cars surrounded the home. CoCo was crying and screaming about something as the tears cascaded down her face. Her nanny stood in the driveway hopeless clinging to the hand of a cute little boy that I assumed was CoCo and Cass's son. This shit made me hate Cass even more. I guess CoCo the house and all that shit she had was in Cass's name, or she was a part of whatever they had going on cause how did they know to come for her. I prayed they didn't come for me next, but I hadn't done shit. The truck I had was gone, the only thing that truly linked me to him was my place of employment; or should I say my previous place of employment since now I knew I was going to have to find another job.

The only thing left for me to do was drive home and get my thoughts together after I changed out of these pissy ass clothes. As soon as I made it to the house and parked in the driveway my phone was ringing. "Hello?" I answered.

"Girlllll!" Nicole squealed. "You better be lucky your ass wasn't there today cause the Feds came and raided the whole spot. They shut that shit down. We all had to leave and I'm not even sure if we can go back."

"What? You foreal?" I asked while shaking my damn head. I didn't even wanna tell her bout the shit I had just went through.

"Yep, they even arrested those big stupid ass bodyguard niggas that be with Cass, but they let me go though. I ain't have shit to do with what they got going on. I left that shit on two wheels cause girl that's not where I was trying to be. I'm about to find me another job."

"You and me both." I told her. "I gotta go Nicole. I'll keep in touch." I told her before hanging up and making my way in the house to wash myself up real good while praying my parents were sleep. I didn't see anybody when I walked inside, but when I came out the shower my mama was up and walking from the kitchen holding a cup of water looking at me like I was crazy. Instead of giving her eye contact, I continued to my room.

"You wanna tell me why you walked in here smelling like piss LeLe? I smelled that loud ass shit all in the hallway when you walked in."

I sat on the bed and sighed before pulling out all of my money counting it right in front of her after I slipped on a big shirt and some comfortable shorts. "Long story ma. I really don't wanna talk about." I was getting annoying with her even just standing over me cause I seriously wasn't in the mood. I was worried.

"Um hmmm." She said with her nose turned up. "Ya'll gon' learn about keeping all these secrets. They come back and bite you in the ass every single time. I'm not gone let ya'll kids drive me crazy." She turned and walked away but I could hear her still rambling. "I'mma go tend to my damn husband cause ya'll too damn grown for me."

I heard her door slam after that. I put the money up and pulled out the laptop before powering it on. I needed to fill out some job applications and I had to do it as soon as possible. Unfortunately it had to be low budget jobs that would hire a felon to the extent of my crime. It was times like this I'd call Abbey first or be somewhere on her couch crying and shit, sucked that I couldn't do that right now and this made me realize that just maybe I did need to talk to her. I needed her even if she didn't think I did. I just couldn't get down with her messing around with my little brother.

Chapter 2

Abbey Daniels

I pulled up to Kim's house and was greeted with Majestic outside leaned up against his car smoking a joint out in the public like the shit was legal. He had blown my damn phone up back-to-back all damn day and when I finally answered, all he could tell me was to meet him here. I hopped out of my car and threw my hands up in the air. "What now Majestic? You know I work with clients. I can't just run at the drop of a dime while you calling me like you're my man." I sucked my teeth.

He just stared at me. "It's been three weeks."

"For?" I quizzed.

He shook his head. "Ion understand how the fuck ya'll can say ya'll 'real' friends and you don't even know ya girl been missing for three weeks."

"Well how do you know? Last I heard, yo the dicks locked yo ass up. When the hell did you even get out?" I heard all about the raid the Feds did. Swept all they ass up. Word had gotten out all in the streets. I heard a few of them got out and Majestic must've been in that few. They didn't care about his ass anyway. They usually wanted the big fish, that's probably why Trey and Cass hadn't gotten out yet. When Trell told me about it, I couldn't believe it. I was so glad that LeLe hadn't got caught up in that shit as well.

"Yeah well, I'm out now and Kim's ass is missing. Per the rent office she don't even live here no more. She broke her lease and bounced." He scratched his head and took another pull off his joint before tossing it. "Only kinda muhfuckas I know who move like that is muhfuckas that's hiding or running from something."

I swallowed a hard lump in my throat and furrowed my brows. "Are you sure?" I asked.

"The fuck, I wouldn't have called you here if I wasn't. Go ask ya'self. I'm tellin' you what the people said."

I exhaled and walked away with my heart beating fast as fuck. If Kim had just moved out the blue that means she didn't plan on telling Majestic, nor LeLe what she'd done and that was fucked up on so many levels that she would just leave without saying shit and having me walk around with this shit on my chest. I slowly walked away from him to get back in my car. "Let me make some calls. I'll call you." I told him.

Majestic didn't say shit else to me, he simply watched me drive away. The fact that he was so interested in Kim had me shook. Obviously he was feeling something for her because he wouldn't keep popping up if he didn't; I didn't give a shit how bad he tried to disguise it. I waited until I left her old complex to pull out my phone and call her number only to find it was disconnected. Although I was pissed to the third degree with her, that didn't mean she should pull no shit like this. After the shit she'd done, I shouldn't even care about her ass but I couldn't help it. I called Karter next to see if I could get some answers cause God knows, when I saw Kim I was fucking her ass up again for pulling this shit. Like, bitch face your problems and own your shit. This was such a coward ass move on her behalf.

"Hey Queen." She said as soon as she picked up.

"Karter. Where the fuck is Kim? Did you know she's been missing for weeks now? Don't tell me you don't know. That's your damn sister."

"Calm down." She told me. Little Barbie was in the back whining and she was trying to calm her down as well. Sometimes it slipped my mind that she was still a brand new mommy. "Now, I don't know where she is; but if you're concerned and want to know if she's okay she is. She's apparently getting her life together."

"Getting her life together where?" I asked. "Is she up there with you?"

"I wouldn't dare let Kim live in my house. That wouldn't work. I haven't spoken much to her. I only know she's okay. She won't talk to me a lot, she's become really good friends with Emily though, which is strange but whatever. Emily will be Emily. She doesn't want to turn her back on Kim because she's my sister but I keep trying to explain to Emily that Kim has a black heart, she isn't me."

"Yeah, well, like the rest of us she probably feels sorry for her ass." I turned on 27th avenue trying to beat the traffic in frustration. Had Majestic let me go the fuck home after work I wouldn't be caught up in all this damn traffic. "If you so happen to talk to her little coward ass you tell her she better call me or else it's on. I'll let all her shit loose."

"Will do my sister. I have to get back to Barbie. Talk to you soon." She rushed me off the phone before hanging up. Karter was still holding on to this black and

16

proud shit, but whatever made her happy with her little life than whatever.

I felt my stomach growling on the way home so I stopped by Snapper's and got me a fried shrimp and wing combo with some fries and a fruit punch flop. I think I must've been on two wheels trying to make it home to eat. When I finally pulled up, I rushed inside and locked the door. Before I could even kick my shoes off, Trell was at the door. I knew it was him because he was the only one bold enough to always just show up unannounced. I swung the door open and much to my surprise LeLe was standing there staring me in the face with a McDonald's uniform on. "Can I come in or you just gonna stare at me?" She walk pass me without me actually inviting her inside. The loud smell of grease and fried food followed behind her when she walked in.

I had no idea she was working at McDonald's now. That was definitely a huge downgrade from Jazzy's. Locking the door, I went and took a seat across from her at the island in the middle of my kitchen floor and pulled my food from out of the plastic bag. LeLe looked like her nerves were wrecked as her right leg shook. I could tell she had a lot of shit on her mind. After five minutes, she still hadn't said anything. "So you gonna say something LeLe? Is everything okay?"

She got up and started pacing. "Hell no everything isn't okay Abbey. That fuck nigga Cass confiscated my truck. He banned me from working at Jazzy's too, 'AFTER' he gave someone else the head chef job and then cut my pay. The Feds then ran down on him while I was trying to confront his ass and I almost went down too. hadn't it been for Trey hiding me in the floor, I would've went down."

She was going so damn fast I had to catch up. "Wait what?"

"Yeah, just keep up cause it's a lot. Listen a little faster Abbey damn." She sucked her teeth and kept going. "So then I went to CoCo's house to give her the heads up and let her know Trey got arrested, and since he don't fuck with her like that for her not listening to him about staying away from Cass, I knew he probably wouldn't call her. Hell, I figured maybe she could tell their parents or something."

"Who is CoCo?" I asked confused like hell.

"CoCo is Trey's sister, and she's also Cass's baby mama. They got a lil son together or whatever. That's why I cut him off cause I went to visit CoCo and she told me everything. That's when the nigga started tripping on me and switched everything up. Oh, and his name is actually Poochie; well his street name and that restaurant is just a front. he's using it to clean his drug money."

"Whew chile!" I shook my head. "This is too much LeLe." I mean, Trey had mentioned the shit about Cass going down for drugs and shit but I didn't know the rest.

"Yeah I know. So anyway, I get to CoCo's house and her shit is surrounded and she's in cuffs being taken away so I never got to tell her shit. I had to go to find me another job quick so here I am, working at fucking McDonald's until I can find something better." She finally stopped and exhaled. "I'm so worried about Trey cause he hasn't gotten out yet and it isn't like I can go see him."

I squint my eyes. "Why are you so pressed about Trey like he's your man. Am I missing something?" I knew we hadn't spoken in what seems like forever but she better had spilled the beans if it's something else that was going on.

"Did you not hear what I said? He saved me from going to jail when he could've easily saved himself Abbey. That's why I'm worried."

"He's a bold man cause ion know if I would've been able to do that." I walked next to her placing my hand on her shoulder. "I'm sorry it went down like that. I had a feeling in my gut that fucking Cass wasn't right. The nigga was just being too nice."

"Exactly." She told me flopping down on the couch. "I'm just stressed the fuck out. I'm not even speaking with your ass but here I am venting and rambling and you're right here listening."

I nod my head in agreement with what she was saying. "Real friends don't fold LeLe, may bend a little but we ain't gone fold. For what it's worth, the situation with Trell and me…"

She cut me off. "I don't wanna talk about that right now. Don't even wanna think about it cause ya'll so fucking wrong. I just don't wanna talk about that."

"We don't have to." I told her contemplating on whether or not I should tell her about the situation with Kim. Since Kim got missing, I probably should. I mean, I didn't want to seem like I'm the one always holding the secrets but at the same time, I didn't wanna keep hurting my friend. "LeLe, I've been meaning to talk to you about something." I let her know feeling scared all over again. "Have a glass of wine with me."

She frowned. "Nah, ion want no wine. What happened?"

"Please?" I begged with my eyes. "One glass, just one." At this point I was desperate and I needed her to relax.

"No Abbey, just spit it out. What happen? At this point I don't think it's nothing I can't fucking handle. My life has been fucked up for the last few years. I think you know that better than anybody else."

If she didn't want the drink then I wasn't going to force her, so I took me a shot of patron straight to the head and frowned my face at the burning sensation as it went down. "It's no easy way to say this so I'mma just say it. Kim is snorting coke for one, and for two, we went to visit Karter since she had the baby and we were surprised to find out that not only is her fiancé white, but she's a woman. Karter's ass has been living this big ol' lie all this time that's why she's been so secretive. They had the artificial insemination done."

LeLe's eyes got big as hell. "I knew it was something. Even when she sent me the picture, that baby looked white as hell." She shook her head. "That wasn't even shit to lie about. She's probably ashamed cause all that shit she be preaching about being black and proud of it. Now Kim on the other hand, coke?"

"Yeah and she was out of control but this is what I really need to tell you. I was giving her the opportunity, but since she got missing I'm going to say it. Brace yourself LeLe."

I could see the worry in her eyes. "Just say it."

I thought it was pretty sad that disappointment was becoming a huge part of her life. She was surrounded by more disappointment than happiness. "Kim and me went to visit Karter when she had the baby and their mama was there. Long story short the shit was a mess. They got into it real bad about their mama not believing Kim when she told her that her stepfather was raping her when she was younger."

I watched LeLe's hand fly up to her mouth wearing a horrific look on her face as she gasped.

I nod my head. "Yep and that's not it. That put Kim in a real fucked up headspace so she was outside talking to Karter and I overheard her breaking down about everything coming clean. She was saying something about wanting to release her demons." I found myself rambling trying to go in circles at this point.

"Abbey! Stop rambling and just tell me."

This shit was making me nervous like I was a child about to get my ass beat. I was so damn nervous my red skin was flushed and my eyes were watery as hell.

"Damn Abbey is it that bad?" She asked with her face screwed up. Next thing I knew she was in my face shaking me by the shoulders. "Just fucking say it!"

Without thinking twice about it I squeezed my eyes shut refusing to look at her and just blurted it out. "You didn't kill Malik! Kim used to fuck Malik before he got with you but he made her promise not to ever tell it! She got mad because he chose you and not her so when he proposed to you that just took her over the top! The night he died, she spiked ya'll drinks! She wanted to hurt you both, she didn't want anybody to die!" I slowly opened my eyes. The look that LeLe gave me with the hurt in her eyes nearly killed me.

She slowly walked away from me and flopped back down on the couch propping her hand up under her chin looking defeated. Her lips trembled and her skin looked pale. "She… wait…" she cleared her throat trying to make sense of what I had just told her. "I lost the love of my life and 2 ½ years of my life behind Kim and her jealousy? I can't even…" She started gasping for air having a panic attack. "I can't breath Abbey."

I rushed to the Kitchen and grabbed a bottle of water forcing her to drink it. "Drink this LeLe… now!" She gobbled the water down and then held her chest.

LeLe broke down throwing her head in my lap as I listened to the deep howl like cries. I could tell that it came from the depths of her soul. For the next thirty minutes she cried while I stroked her long hair and her back consoling her. "I can't believe Kim. I'm gonna kill that bitch. I'll kill her! How could she do me like this? I didn't know about her and Malik! I didn't know!"

"I know you didn't LeLe. None of this shit is your fault and it doesn't change the way Malik felt about you. That's just Kim and her own fucked up ways. Hurt people hurt people LeLe. Hell, I even beat her ass when she admitted all of this. I haven't spoken to her since and now she's missing."

"That bitch better be missing cause I promise she's gone have to see me! Fuck Kim. From this day on that bitch is dead to me! That bitch took the biggest part of my heart from me. I lost my child behind her; I lost my life behind her." She stood up looking at her appearance. "I'm flipping burgers and frying fries everyday. I'm not knocking nobody hustle but I had so much shit I wanted to do."

"I know LeLe... I know." I agreed. "This shit is fucked up, but it's how you move on from here. You can't let life win."

"Does Majestic know about this?" She asked. "That man and his mama fucking hate me! They hate because of some shit Kim started!"

I hated to break some more news to her but I had to. "Kim is fucking Majestic and I think she has feelings for him too. Matter-of-fact I think they have feelings for each other to be honest with you. He's the one that told me she broke her lease and vanished. I personally think this is the reason she vanished. If Majestic knew the truth, he'd kill her."

"That trifling fucking bitch!" She spat. "I'm gonna have to talk to him. He can believe me or not but I need them to know the truth. Will you help me tell them the truth? It makes more sense coming from somebody who actually heard it."

"Absolutely." I told her. "Whenever you're ready we can do it."

LeLe grabbed her keys and nod her head. Using the back of her hands she wiped the tears away from both of her red and now swollen eyes. "I'll let you know when. I have to go." She told me.

I walked her to the door feeling terrible. I knew she wasn't really feeling me either, but no matter what, we always have been there for each other and this time was no different. Even with our disagreements. I watched LeLe get in her Nissan and pull off before going to take my shower. My poor chicken wings and shrimp that I didn't get to finish was sitting on the island cold as hell so I just tossed it out since I no longer had an appetite. I felt like a weight had been lifted off of my chest since LeLe knew the truth now.

After I got out the shower I threw on my robe and curled up under the covers but not before popping me a Percocet. My damn head was pounding so badly. I pulled out my phone and opened up to Instagram to see what the hell Trell was up to. Every time he tried to have a real conversation with me I curved him like I was just too busy and for the past few days I hadn't heard from him. I could tell he was getting over my shit but what I wasn't expecting to see a sexy ass picture of himself and all the little young hoes under there sweating him. One particular comment stood out to me. It was some bitch telling him he was a king and, left 50 million damn heart eye emojis.

Of course being a female I clicked on her profile to see who the hell she was. When I saw her repost a picture of Trell on her page and captioned it with a simple heart; my heart dropped. Like what the hell? I knew how I was supposed to feel, but I couldn't help what I felt and the shit made me sad. I damn sho was finna shut this shit down. I immediately called him only to not get an answer. Sent him a text too and no reply. If that's how he wanted to play the game then it was all good. Fuck it.

Chapter 3

Latrell 'Trell' Wells

I ignored Abbey's call and walked into the strip club solo. I'd been in my own zone lately. I didn't have time to play these games with Abbey. I laid my feelings on the line so if this wasn't what she wanted then fuck it. It is what it is. I told her, either she was gone let me love her or watch me love somebody else. Bumping through the crowd I walked to the bar and told the bartender 'Redd' that I wanted my own personal bottle of Remy and waited for her to bring it. I didn't need a section and all that other fancy shit. No bottle girls, no sparkles flying; just me, and my bottle.

I normally didn't go to places like this without my gun on me so I shot the security at the door a dolla to let me come in with it. I'd rather been safe than sorry and a nigga wasn't bout to catch me slippin', fuck that. After I tipped Redd, I took my bottle, my bucket of ice with my plastic cups, and sat in my own section. I wasn't on the shit the other niggas was on in here. I wasn't here for dances and bitches shakin' ass in my face. I wasn't even throwin' no money around cause every dollar counted at this point. With Poochie locked up wasn't shit moving right now and niggas was getting weary not knowing what to expect.

Even if the nigga was home. I was done with that shit. After my mama told me the way he did LeLe; I had no respect for that nigga. Fuck'em. Majestic was tryna make a lil somethin' shake but I couldn't focus on that. I myself was still trying to figure out how the fuck that nigga get out and everybody else was still locked up. I couldn't focus too much on that though cause I had bigger shit going on.

Graduation was less than a week away and I must admit, I'm surprised I made it this far. I felt some kinda way with the NFL drafts approaching too. If God had any love for me he'd put me in the first round picks cause Lord knows all I wanted to do was take care of my mama. Los Angeles Rams would be sweet. That's something I'd been hiding from everyone cause I didn't wanna get my hopes up but draft night; I wanted everyone there.

"You good? You need anything baby?" Redd came over and checked on me. I used to fuck her back in the day when we were in high school. Back then she was skinny as fuck and had no kinda shape. She'd had a baby since then though and now she was thick in all the right places. She'd always been pretty too but Redd was a hoe. That pussy had more miles than a Mack truck and if the dollar amount was right she would do circles on the dick.

"I'm good ma." I let her know before sending her on her way. I thought about Leon. It had been a minute since I saw that nigga. I couldn't even lie and say the shit ain't fuck with me cause it did. If I couldn't depend on nobody else I knew I could depend on my brother but him turning on me for a nigga; that shit hurt me more than anything. I would've never put my hands on Leon hadn't he hit me first. He should've been checking that nigga, not me.

Another thing that fucked with me was this 'gay' shit. I don't know how I'm supposed to accept that. Maybe if he would've come talk to me about it then it would've been different, or maybe not. Either way, I didn't like it and the shit is embarrassing as fuck. At the same time, I couldn't see myself allowing nobody to fuck with him about it; that shit wasn't gon' fly with me. I'd put a muhfucka in the ground about my brother but for now, this just how shit had to be.

I looked down at my flashing phone alerting me that I had a text message. Bobbing my head to the music and taking a sip from my cup, I checked the message. One from Tyliyah, a lil chick I had been kickin' it heavy with and the other one was from Abbey telling me to call her. I ignored Abbey's cause she had me fucked up. All she wanted to do was fuck me, hide me, and swallow plan B's every other fucking day. She swallowed so many plan B's they might as well had just put her ass on they payroll. I was sick of that shit. If this is what she wanted, it was her who had to make the effort, not me.

I let Tyliyah know that I was gone stop by her apartment when I left from where I was and left it at that. I sat in this bitch for about an hour observing everything. Wasn't shit like a Miami strip club or the Miami nightlife for that matter, but I wanted more. This wasn't it. Niggas was walking round this bitch looking hood rich but dead ass broke and up in this bitch tryna put on for hoes. I wasn't with that shit though.

When I felt a nice lil buzz, I knew it was time for me to go. I would never let myself get too fucked up. For one, I wouldn't give a nigga the chance to catch me slippin' and for two, I would never forget what happened with LeLe and Malik after getting too fucked up in the club. Nah, fuck that.

On the way out to the car, I stopped and grabbed me a rib sandwich before I left. The closer I got to Tyliyah's house. The more Abbey clouded my mind. Her silly ass was too busy worried about LeLe but I knew my sister. LeLe was gone be good regardless. I turned up the music in my whip even louder tryna drown her ass out of my mind. Not even a block away from Tyliyah's house and my mama was calling me. "Everything good?" I asked her.

"No, something is wrong with my car and I need you to go to the 24-hour Walgreens to pick up George's prescription for me."

"Aiight, give me a minute." I told her. "I'm coming."

"Hurry up." She hung up in my face.

I just tossed the phone in the passenger seat and shook my head. I pulled up in the visitors spot and hopped out. Before I could even knock on the door it was opening. "Sup Liyah?" I walked in the dark apartment. The only light came from the lamp she had lit in the living room along some fruity smelling ass candles she had lit. Liyah was a feisty lil thing and pretty as fuck but she wasn't Abbey though. Liyah was short and stacked. She had the prettiest chocolate skin and full lips. She wore her natural hair in long dread locks that she normally had colored and styled in something pretty. The only thing I didn't like about her was her jealous ass ways. No matter how nice looking she was, she had a habit of always thinking somebody just wanted to fuck her over. Liyah was real insecure about herself.

"What took you so long to get here?" She asked pouting and I knew she was about to start.

Leaning up against the wall, I just stared at her at first admiring her beauty before I said anything else. "Don't start Liyah, I didn't come over here for all this tonight."

"Good." She said pressing her short frame up against mine while standing on her tippy toes to kiss me. "Cause I don't wanna argue anyway. I just want some dick." She licked her lips and took a step back to unzip my jeans and pull my dick out of my boxers. The minute I felt her soft lips wrapped around my dick I closed my eyes and relaxed with one hand on top of her head guiding her. I knew I said I wanted to be with Abbey, but it was times like this that had me asking if I really wanted to give up the single life. For her, I would.

After I satisfied mine and Liyah's needs, I made my way to Walgreens to grab George prescription and then stopped to Miami Subs to grab a grilled wing platter and some salads just in case they was hungry. I had to admit that I hated pulling up and not seeing Leon's car or being able to chop it up with him and shit. I walked in the room and sat the food down with the pills for George. Him and ma Dukes was up watching T.V.

I'm glad George was feeling better. He had been up and walking around for the past couple of weeks but he still didn't fully have his energy back. I had to figure some shit out and figure it out quick cause while my mama was living off her pension and with George out of work I knew soon finances would be an issue that's why I covered as much as I could without them having to go in their pockets. I learned to move smart. Instead of splurging the money I'd made with Majestic, I put my shit up for a rainy day. Looked like these were the rainy days.

"Thanks son, you sho'll know yo mama cause I was about to send you on a food run next." She opened the blue cheese and poured it over the chicken wing before taking a bite out of it.

George went for the salad. "Thanks buddy, I appreciate this. How much I owe you for the medicine?" He asked.

Shit cost a dolla but I didn't want him to pay me back. Nigga took care of me all my life. "Don't worry bout it." I told him yawning before walking out to take me a shower. I had to walk past Leon's empty room on the way. Can't believe my nigga actually went and got his own place. I'm not sure if I was ready to talk to him, but I did miss the nigga. Couldn't even lie.

Chapter 4

Kimberly 'Kim' Laws

"I'm trying so hard Emily." I complained over the phone. "Everyday I'm trying not to leave this place. They treat me like a fucking child and I'm tired of talking my personal business in these groups in front of all these strangers."

"But is it working?" She asked sounding like she had a lot going on in her background. "Listen, you're so lucky right now. You've been more blessed than a lot of other people because they don't have the opportunity to do this and I'm paying good money for you to be at one of the most top of the line facilities that will care for you and your unborn baby."

As soon as she said that I felt bad. Looking down at my little pudge I couldn't believe that I was nearly five months. When I missed my period, I assumed I was early on in my pregnancy because I hadn't had any other symptoms prior to this. I still knew it was Majestic's though cause he was the only one of my niggas I didn't mind not using a condom with. I was still in awe that this entire time I had a little person growing in me and it never showed. I never felt anything. I didn't gain any weight at all; and just I believe if I had any kind of symptoms that I didn't even notice because I was always high and drinking. "You're right Emily. I'm sorry for being so damn bitchy, I just can't help it."

"No it's fine. I completely understand. You're pregnant and you're moody."

"Yeah, I know." I told her looking over my shoulder at the counselor. Every one was piling up in one room getting ready to have our daily meeting. I knew I was fucked up but these bitches in here were on some other shit. They had real issues, I didn't think I could meet a person who had deeper issues than mine. At first I wouldn't even talk to nobody but I got cool with one person. A girl named Lolita who's the same age as me. Our stories were so much alike that it was scary. "Well look Emily, I have to go so kiss Barbie for me and tell Karter I said hey."

"Will do sweet cakes. Oh, and happy birthday." She told me before hanging up the phone in a rush to get back to work. Karter and me still didn't speak much. I just think after all my confessions that Karter really didn't wanna be involved with any of it. Her main focus was always her new daughter and I had to respect that. I took a long deep breath and walked to my little room. I wasn't in the birthday spirit at all. Wasn't shit to be happy about besides the baby I was carrying. I decided that I didn't wanna know the sex until it was time to deliver. I wanted it to be a surprise.

I changed my clothes into something comfortable and drag my feet to our daily meeting taking my sweet little time cause I didn't even wanna go. I thought about just laying under the covers telling them I was sick but they always wanted to have me see the nurse and shit any time I claimed sick and I didn't have time to be faking it today. Lolita stood at the door all happy rushing me to come inside. "Come on girl, what's taking you so long? You made it to see another year. Perk up."

"I'm coming Lo." I told her cause I hated saying Lolita. Sounded like the name of an old person and she wasn't hardly that. She should've kicked her mama's ass for naming her that in this generation. Lo was the same exact height as me and very pretty. She wore her hair cut low in a fade and kept it colored all different kind of colors depending on how she felt. Her body was nice but her brown butterscotch skin wore many visible marks on it from a hard life. Just like me she used to snort dope too trying to hide her pain.

Hell, her mama willingly allowed her stepfather to rape her until she eventually became pregnant with his child at the age of seventeen who she ended up giving up for adoption cause she couldn't bare to keep looking at a child that reminded her of him. Because of that, her stepfather went to jail and her mama too for soliciting a minor. Lo didn't have any family like that besides her man Demarcus. She married him when she was twenty-two years old and they had their own baby girl but he couldn't fix her deep rooted issues so here she was getting the help she needed in order to keep her family together.

Sometimes when him and their little daughter would come visit I would feel a twinge of jealousy watching the three of them together knowing that would never be me. I knew that when I told Majestic the truth about Malik, he probably wouldn't even let me live and that's something I've been trying to come to peace with every single day. Another part of me just didn't want to ever have to say anything at all. Why couldn't I just raise my baby and never have to go back and face those demons? The more I asked myself that, the more I answered my own questions. I had to make this right for LeLe. It did hurt me to know that friendship would forever be over.

I had managed to fuck over the same people who would've done anything for me. "Kim! Come on!" Lolita said again snapping me out of my thoughts. I picked up my pace. Hell, they could've started the meeting without me for all I cared. I had nothing to talk about. When I made it inside of the room I was shocked when everyone yelled "Surprise!"

"What the hell?" I looked around with my hand over my mouth wondering how they were able to do all of this right up under my nose. The room was decorated with yellow, pink, and gold balloons. There was a plastic tablecloth on the table along with confetti, a birthday cake, and some finger foods. "Omggg ya'll." I smiled feeling really moved by this. "Ya'll tricked me." I giggled. "Thank you so much. This is beautiful."

I walked around the room giving everyone hugs and thanking them. Nothing about these women in the room with me was perfect. They each had a story to tell and to the streets I'm sure just like me they were written off from society. To us, we were all we had to build our lives back up, even if it was just for the moment. "Girl this is why I was rushing your ass. Happy Birthday." Lolita hugged me. "Now go give this baby some cake."

"Happy birthday slim!" Everybody else told me since that's what they called me in here. I truly did appreciate this.

As I cut into the cake cutting everyone slices of it, I had another surprise when Emily and Karter walked in. They didn't have the baby with them. Karter looked uneasy but Emily was cool. She had balloons in her hand that she handed me along with a card. "Wowww what are ya'll doing here?" I hugged them both grabbing the balloons. "Thank you so much. Emily you didn't even tell me you were headed up here."

"I wanted…" She stopped and looked at Karter. "No… we wanted to surprise you." She told me.

I gave Karter a soft look. "Thank you for coming. I really appreciate this and everything ya'll are doing for me."

"You're welcome sis, but I'm not doing anything for you. It's Emily who's really thinking you will change." She shrugged. "I'm just here for the ride watching it play out."

I wasn't used to Karter being so cold with me but I understood. The old me would've cussed her ass out but since I was trying to work on myself, I didn't go there. Instead, I swallowed hard and pierced my lips together and just nodded my head so I didn't say the wrong shit. "Understood. Would you like some cake?"

"Sure." She shrugged. I sliced two pieces of cake for them both before we went to sit down off to the side by ourselves.

"Where's Barbie?" I asked.

"She's with the nanny." Karter replied picking over the cake. I could tell she was so uninterested in being here. "I didn't want to bring her here around all of these germs with her being so little ya know? This isn't the place for her."

"I get it." I replied.

"I'm glad this place is helping you Kim. Even your spirit seems different." Emily told me munching down on her cake. Her slice was practically gone already.

"Yeah, we get to express ourselves and the counselors help a lot. It was hard at first going through withdrawals of not being able to have the one devil that took over me so long, but now it's just the part of dealing with the trauma ya know? I be talking my shit about being here but this is the perfect place for me."

"I'm very happy for you. I'll make sure I drop off more toiletries and hygiene supplies next week." She stood up looking at her watch. "I have to get Karter home to Barbie and get back to work. I have a really big case I'm working on."

It made me sad they were leaving so soon but I understood. I hugged them both and thanked them again for coming before watching them leave. Instead of dwelling on shit I had to pray it would fall in place and just decided to enjoy the rest of the little party they had going for me. My stomach was growling something bad so the first thing I did was grabbed a slice of pizza. They didn't allow us to have our cell phones in here so we had to use the facility phones. I wanted to call Majestic, and Abbey, and LeLe so many times even if it were just to hear their voices but I knew I couldn't so I didn't.

When it was all said and done, I lay in my bed alone just wondering if everything could've been different. I truly wished I could turn back the hands of time. I would've reported my stepfather to the laws but I didn't out of fear. I would've just accepted the fact that Malik never really wanted me, but I didn't. Instead, I allowed my jealousy to take over and now there was no turning back. "Ms. Laws, you have a phone call." My counselor Mrs. Andrews stood at the door briefly to tell me that before walking away.

I got up and walked on over to the office where the phone was wondering who was calling me because the only two people that knew I was here was Emily and Karter. They knew not to tell anybody else. I snatched the phone up off the receiver. "Hello?" I answered.

"Happy birthday Kimberly." My mama told me sounding really dry. My skin crawled hearing her voice. The little hairs on the back of my neck instantly stood up.

"What do you want? Why are you even calling me?" I frowned. "Who told you I was here?"

"Oh please, you know Karter isn't going to lie to me. You should be glad somebody wants to tell your sour ass happy birthday."

I sucked my teeth. "I'm about to hang the fuck up. You got two seconds to say what you want."

"Oh I wont be long, no worries. Just thought you should know I'll be trying to seek custody of my grandchild since it's clear you're not fit to be a parent. Keep that in mind."

"Bitch!" I spat. "Over my fucking dead ass body. You must be out of your fucking mind if you think I'd let my child stay up under a roof with you and your fucking child molesting ass husband! Don't you ever fucking call here again!" I hung up in her face. My entire body was shaking. How dare she! Old evil unfit ass bitch.

"Is everything okay?" Mrs. Andrews asked watching me from the door of the office.

"Hell no! Put her ass on the block list. Ion want no calls from her and she can't ever come here to see me!" I marched out crying. This pregnancy shit had me super emotional. I wasn't beat for this shit. I walked back to my bed and laid down. I don't know who the fuck she even thought she was. This was even more of a reason why I needed to at least talk to Majestic, I just didn't know how.

If anything should ever happen to me I wanted my baby to be with his or her family. A family that would love the baby. Not just anybody, and my mama was literally a anybody. She had fucked up my whole day and now I didn't even wanna be here now that she knew where I was. I would be leaving here sooner than expected. Where I would go after? I didn't know. I needed a job up here cause I couldn't depend on Emily forever, she had done enough for me. I missed decorating already but I knew that I didn't have any clientele up here and being pregnant nobody would hire me. I didn't even have any clients to train or anything.

I marched back to the office and called Emily. "Karter told my mama I was here and now she's threatening to come after my baby. She can't get custody of my baby Emily. I can't deliver here. I need to get my shit together so my child could have some stability when he or she gets here."

"Wow." Emily sighed. "I didn't know she did that Kim. I apologize about that. I can understand your frustration. Between you and I, I don't really care for her that much either. You can always start a new life here."

I thought briefly for a second. I was running but I couldn't hide forever. "Um I have a few more sessions. I want to leave after that."

"I tell you what, if you finish those sessions I'll let you work at my firm as a receptionist. You can be my personal assistant but keep in mind that this is my business Kim. If you do anything to tarnish my business I'll never speak to you nor help you again." She chuckled. "I'm serious."

"I promise I wont do that. I'll be on my best behavior. I swear." That was fucked up that everybody painted such an ugly picture of me and didn't trust me. I couldn't blame nobody but myself. I'd work at Emily's firm for the rest of my pregnancy and after that, I was going back home. I needed to fix this.

Chapter 5

Leon Wells

I watched LeLe clean and dust around my lil spot before she took all the stuff she used her own money to purchase to put my bathroom together for me. Today was graduation day. Trell, Kevin, and myself were scheduled to graduate this evening and I didn't know how this shit was gon' go cause I hadn't even spoken to Kevin nor Trell in a while now. I wanted to talk to Kevin but it wasn't fair for me to keep bringing myself in his life while fighting my demons. He knew what he wanted so he wasn't the problem, I was. I'm glad I moved cause it gave me time to really get to learn myself.

I sat on the couch and thought about the money that I had left. I'm glad I managed to pay my lil rent up for six months cause after the dicks came and picked up Poochie and his crew, shit had been slow and wasn't shit movin'. Even Majestic wasn't making no moves cause niggas was scared. I knew it was gone be a matter of time before I had to go ahead and put my degree to use. I just didn't know exactly where yet. My passion had always been Forensic Science, niggas in the hood thought I was only taking up that degree cause it looked good. In reality, I was hood cause of the environment I grew up in but I had other dreams. Trell's dream was always to play in the NFL. Me on the other end, I never gave a fuck about going to the NBA. Nigga just wanted to work a good job, settle down and be happy, that's it.

I snapped from my thoughts watching LeLe again and how focused she was. I couldn't even lie and say I didn't admire her hustle cause I did. I knew one day great things was gone happen for LeLe cause she was a hard worker and I knew she was busting her ass now working two jobs to save her money. She was at McDonald's by the day and Taco Bell by the night. I watched baby sis hustle day in and day out. I knew this wasn't her dream but she made the best of it and as long as I had breath in my body, I was gone make sure I did what I could to help her get that restaurant she wanted. I knew Trell would too.

"You aiight? Why yo face all balled up?" I asked her now standing in the doorframe of the bathroom.

She continued working but she openly talk to me. "Have you seen or heard from Trey?"

"Nah, ain't nobody heard shit since he got locked up. To be honest ion even think we would know if he was out. That's one strategic nigga right there. I can guarantee they ain't even have shit on him and if they did, he got one good ass lawyer. Why?" I quizzed wondering why she was even stressing over him.

"Just asking." She shrugged wiping the sweat from her forehead using the back of her hand. "You like your bathroom? I'm bout done." She smiled.

"Yeah, I like it. But something is up with you. What's bothering you sis? Yo ass been spaced out every time I've seen you for the past few weeks."

"Yeah well, if a broken heart was a person, it would be me." She sighed. "I don't know why the Lord thought I was strong enough to handle all the shit I've been handed but he can give me a break now. I've endured enough hurt. I can't take it no more." She shook her head.

I knew it was a lot of shit she wasn't telling me, but I wasn't going to force her cause when she was ready I knew she would talk to me. "God handles the toughest battles to his strongest soldiers sis. You've been through the hardest parts already so it ain't nothing you can't handle." I placed a kiss on her forehead. Although LeLe is the big sister, at times I felt I needed to play the big brother role.

"Yeah, I guess. So you excited about graduation? I really hope ya'll act right around each other tonight."

"Who?"

"I'm talking about all ya'll. You, Trell, and Kevin. This is a big night."

"It is what it is. It'll come together sis. Don't even worry about that." I told her. "I'mma talk to Kevin and I'mma try to talk to Trell too."

"Good. Well I'm gonna go home and shower and stuff. We only have a few hours so I'll see you there." She reached up kissing my cheek. "Proud of you." She smiled before grabbing her stuff walking out.

When LeLe left, I was able to take me a nap and then woke up about an hour and a half before it would be time to go since I still had to shower and put my dress clothes on. When I was finished I looked in the mirror and admired how I looked. I couldn't even front, I was one good looking ass nigga. I could easily see why anybody would have a problem with me being bisexual. That's what I came up with. If anybody was to ask me how I felt about a woman, yes, I was still somewhat attracted to women. However, my feelings and my heart were with Kevin.

Nigga wasn't tryna live in the dark no more or be hurting people and shit cause it wasn't right. Being on my own these last couple of months made me realize that.

When I was satisfied that I had everything, I walked out and locked up. The parking lot for the graduation was packed. As soon as I walked in front of the building LeLe, George, my mama, Trell, some chick that he was with, Abbey, and a few more family and friends were all snapping pictures. "Come on over here." George said spotting me first. The old man looked good, almost new again despite the weight he'd lost.

As soon as he said that, all eyes were on me. I didn't really know what to say but I didn't wanna make the shit even more awkward than it was so I walked on over to them and gave him a hug. "Looking good pops." I told him. I hugged my mama next. "Sup ma." I spoke. I hadn't seen her since the day I moved out.

She looked up at me with tears in her eyes. "I haven't seen you in forever boy. I've been calling you."

"We will talk." I told her. I spoke to Trell next with a simple head nod. He did the same and went right back to pictures. LeLe and Abbey were flicking it up but they both stopped to speak to me. Abbey had a disturbing look on her face but I couldn't make out what the look was all about.

"Let me get a picture with you." LeLe squealed. "Here Abbey, take this picture." Abbey used LeLe's phone to snap the picture. "I need one with me, you, and Trell now."

She pulled me over to where Trell was and stood in between us both. Shit felt weird not clapping it up with my twin on some shit we both worked so hard toward but for the sake of LeLe, we took the picture. After that, we had to head inside so everyone could get seated before it started. On the inside, I saw Kevin talking to his family. He took one look at me like he wanted to say something but instead he gave me a simple wave and a smile. The connection between us was crazy as we both had a quiet conversation with each other. If I could communicate it aloud it was 'I miss you' and a 'I miss you too' kind of thing.

Since we were seated in alphabetical order, Trell and me had to sit right next to each other. We did that, but we didn't speak one word to each other. When they called Kevin's name to accept his degree, Trell didn't have an reaction at all. He didn't say shit. I still clapped for him and when they called Trell right before me, I clapped for him too. this here was a big achievement in our lives. I'd always celebrate this. I was next after him and it felt damn good walking the stage.

After the fact, we took more pictures. This time though, I had to take pictures with my mama and with George too. "We're having a family celebration dinner at the house after this. You make sure you're there son. I have some things to say, to everybody." He winked at me and walked off.

"Are you coming over to eat?" My mama asked me. She didn't seem as genuine as George though. To me it was one of those I'm extending the invite just so you cant say I didn't tell you.

I looked at her sideways. "Yeah, I'm comin'." I assured her, cause I had some shit I needed to get off my chest too.

I looked around for LeLe and Abbey. When I found them it looked like they were in the middle of an uncomfortable conversation. "I don't care, you shouldn't have been fucking him anyway. He can bring who he wants around." LeLe told Abbey looking agitated.

Abbey noticed me coming and decided not to say what she originally wanted to say I guess. "We'll talk in the car." She told her. "What's up Leon? Congrats baby." She hugged me. I didn't have no hard feelings toward Abbey, even when I found out that she igged Trell on to beat Kevin's ass. I respected her for not telling my business when she could've easily went and told everybody what was going on with me.

"I appreciate that." I replied. "I'll see ya'll at the house. I need to tie up some loose ends here."

When they all left, I went and found Kevin, he was with his family taking pictures. "Can I talk to you real quick?" I asked him before smiling at his family. "How ya'll doing?"

They all were friendly as hell when they spoke back. They weren't too fazed by me grabbing Kevin by the hand to lead him away either. "Congratulations Leon. You did it." He smiled. "I don't want you to think I have any hard feelings toward you because I don't. I have to accept some kind of responsibility. It was technically my fault."

"Nah Kevin, we all played a part. It was my fault too cause I played too many games and I didn't make you feel secure cause I wasn't even secure with myself. I think I just drove you crazy cause the games I played. Unfortunately you lashed out at the wrong twin, which caused a whole other problem. I didn't make it no better

46

when I hit my fucking brother in your defense. I allowed my emotions to get the best of me."

"You're right babe. I'm so sorry for that. I caused a complete mess." I watched how his eyes started watering up. Kevin was a water bag when it came to anything he was truly genuine about. "Where do we go from here?" I decided to tell him the truth. Without a care in the world about who was watching. I leaned in and gave him a kiss on the lips even shocking him before pulling back. The look of shock on his face confused me. "What are you doing Leon? That's public affection. Do you know how many people are looking at us?"

"Man fuck them people. I had to fix myself before I could present myself to you again and this is what I want. This is my truth, fuck who don't like it. Even my family cause real love should never waiver." I let him know cause this is just what it was.

"Do you know how long I've waited for this day?" He wiped a tear from his green eye. "I'm so happy for you. Even if it wasn't me, I'd still be happy for you walking in your truth. This is amazing."

"Yep." I chuckled a lil bit. "This what it is and you the one I want. Being around you makes me so much better Kevin. I'm sorry for everything."

"Me too." He grabbed both my hands before hugging me. "Have you told your family yet?"

"I'mma straighten all that out, trust me. I just didn't wanna leave here without making things right with you first. Can I call you later?" I asked him.

He looked over his shoulder at his family who weren't paying us any attention anyway. "I'm going out for dinner with the family but I can call you when we wrap it up."

"Dat's cool."

"Great." He hugged me one more time before getting back to his peoples.

It took me a minute to get back to ma Dukes house but on the way I made sure I stopped and grabbed me a personal bottle of Remy and drank a few sips from the bottle before walking inside. All of the other cars were already here, which let me know I was the last one to arrive. I expected all eyes to be on me when I walked inside but they weren't. Instead, everybody was doing their own thing and the house smelled good as hell.

"I'm glad you made it." George smiled. "The food is almost ready since most of it was prepared early this morning." He said. "Come sit down." He then cleared his throat and stopped everybody from having the conversations they were having. "Now. I need everyone's attention! Turn that music off for a second." He told Trell. Trell immediately turned it down.

Awe shit. I thought to myself. I knew George couldn't wait to speak his peace.

Chapter 6

Abbey Daniels

I was getting ready to leave when George decided he wanted to give a speech when Leon walked in. Trell had the nerve to invite his lil friend over here around the family, which let me know she was definitely somebody he was liking like that. He wasn't acting funny with me or no shit like that but at the same time, he expressed with his body language he wasn't feeling me. The thing that shocked me the most was cause one day I knew this had to happen and it would come to an end. I just didn't know it was going to be like this.

The chick Liyah was cool and all, she wasn't my problem. She didn't even know me so I had no problem with her at all but if this is what Trell wanted it to be than this is just what it was gone be. I guess everybody got their wish. LeLe didn't want me fucking with her brother and now Trell kept his promise and was making me watch him love on somebody else. Like, did my happiness matter at all?

George started talking again snapping me from my thoughts as I sipped on a personal wine cooler. "Now today is an very important day. We are here in front of all the people we love the most; the ones who matter."

"That's right." A lot of other people who I didn't even know started mumbling. I didn't even know half these damn people. The house was packed.

He continued. "I just want to say this. When I first met my children when they were just toddlers, I didn't know what was going to be in store for me. What I did know is I loved my wife and those were her children, which meant everything attached to her was attached to me. If I accepted her, I had to accept them as well, meaning I accepted everything that came with them. I made a promise to never turn my back on them and I stand by that till this very day." He grabbed his wife by the hand. I could tell she wanted him to stop talking cause she looked nervous not knowing what he was going to say in front of all these people. "Now hunny, I didn't judge you for being a single mother of three kids on welfare back then; I stepped up to the plate and loved you anyway. I gave you and those kids my last name." He told her and then looked at LeLe.

"Leandra, when you were in your teens, you gave me the hardest time I'd ever had in my life. A lot of times I sat in that very room back there and contemplated about leaving this house because the kids I worked so hard for didn't even respect me. I didn't judge you for that, I prayed about it and worked with you. When you got locked up that hurt me to my soul. However, I didn't judge you for what you did. I stood by you every step of the way. It didn't change the fact that you're still my daughter and an awesome person."

LeLe smiled. "Yes, you were always there George."

He then looked to Trell. "Latrell…" he started.

Trell threw his hand up. "Nah George, don't be talkin' my business in front of these people. Just know I know all the shit I did and I appreciate you for being there, even the shit ma don't know about." He told him shutting that shit down. I wanted to laugh but I also wanted to slap his ass. That's what attracted me the most to Trell, he spoke his mind and wasn't scared of shit.

"As long as we on the same page." George told him and then he looked to Leon.

"I got'chu son. No matter what you choose to do." He told him and then told everybody else. "This goes for this entire family. We all got demons and some shit we ain't proud of, but who are we to judge one person because of what they choose to do with their lives or the stuff they may go through in life? I don't judge anyone in this room so I'm not about to sit around and allow ya'll to judge my boy. He's been an awesome brother, son, cousin, friend and everything else. He's one of the most dependable men that I know. I don't care what he went out there in the streets and did."

"I appreciate that Pops." Leon nod his head.

Mrs. Wells was wiping tears from her eyes as she squeezed his hand tighter.

"I know you do, but you was wrong son. You put your hands on one person who would kill somebody behind you and I don't care how tough he is, I know it hurts. You owe your brother an apology." He told Leon and then addressed Trell.

"And you son, stop holding on to that anger. Let it go, his sexual preference wont change the kind of brother that he's been to you. If he walked out that door and dies right now you'd probably kill yourself to be buried with him. Now get ya'll shit together right now. Don't you judge your bother cause ya brother never judged you." He grilled them both.

Leon and Trell were both in a stare off at this point, you can hear a pin drop in this bitch that's how quiet it was. I myself was on edge waiting to see what happened with this situation. I was so glad that secrets were unfolding because this was the only way people could truly move on and be happy. Leon was apologetic, Trell on the other hand, I couldn't make out what he wanted to say or do because he just wore this glare on his face. Before anyone could say anything Trell shook his head and stood up. "Nah, fuck this shit, and fuck him too." He walked out of the house causing everyone to gasp, even LeLe.

Mrs. Wells tried to go after him. "No!" I told her. "I got it, let me talk to him."

Liyah stood up and tried to walk out with me. "It's okay, I got it."

I gave her one cold ass glare looking down at her lil short ass. "Sit ya ass down lil mama. You don't know shit about this bond we share. Just sit down."

She didn't know what to say. Her facial expressions said she wanted to say some fly shit out of her mouth but LeLe intervened quickly. "It's cool Liyah, it's family business." She grilled me before I disappeared.

I found Trell sitting on the hood of his car drinking a Corona. Standing right in front of him I used my pointer finger and mushed his ass right in the middle of his forehead. "What's yo fucking problem Trell? That's yo fucking brother!"

"I done told you about putting yo muhfuckin' hands on me Abbey." He warned before taking another swig.

"I don't give a fuck, I'll do it again too! Now what's yo fucking problem! If he's gay he's gay! That doesn't have shit to do with you."

Trell gave me a slight chuckle. "You think that's what this is about? I'm over that shit. If that's what he wanna do that's on his ass."

"So what's the problem."

"You ain't a twin Abbey. You don't even have siblings so you would never understand."

"Make me understand then." I told him losing my damn patience with his ass.

He gave a slight chuckle. "Did you see the look in that nigga eyes when he swung on me that night? Cause if you did you'd know the problem. That nigga love his boyfriend more than he loves me and that's the fucking problem. Leon had hate in his eyes that night. I can't erase that shit if I tried cause it keeps replaying in my mind over and over and over."

I think I was starting to understand now. I squint my eyes and looked at him as I fold both my arms across my chest. "Wait, so that's the real problem. You feel like you're losing your brother to another nigga don't you?"

"And that's a fucked up feeling." He said in a spaced off glare.

Leon walked up scaring the shit out of us both. We were so indulged we hadn't even heard him. "And that'll never happen man. You my bro no matter what. Ain't a soul on this earth can take yo place nigga, we shared the same sac together, this gone always be love." He told Trell with tears in his eyes. "Always."

Trell didn't say anything. His tough ass really wanted to cry and I could tell. "Could ya'll just make up already? Cause this shit is killing everybody like foreal. Just apologize to each other." I said.

Leon's voice was cracking by now but he was desperate to have his brother back. "I apologize man, I really do. I fucked up and I hope you understand that but I'm not too big of a man to apologize, especially to my brother."

Instead of Trell saying anything else, he stood up off the hood and wrapped his arms around his twin brother, the replica of his ass, same exact face. "Love you lil bro. Nigga sorry for passing judgment on you and allat."

"Thank you Jesus!" I smiled looking at the sky. I looked to the door and saw everyone's nosey ass looking out the window but tried to hurry up and rush away when they spotted me looking.

"I'm glad we had this talk Trell. I done came to terms with myself. Nigga don't wanna live this street life or none of that. I wanna be with who I wanna be with and that's Kevin. Ion want nobody to treat the man different cause he got a good heart man. I just want everything to be open."

Trell sighed long and hard as he brushed his hand down his face. "I'mma do this just for you bro. I'mma really try my best. That's my word and that's all I got."

"I respect that." Leon told him.

"Good." I smiled wiping my own tears. "Aww I'm so happyyyyy, but can we go inside now? I'm hungry and I'm freezing."

Trell gave me a side way look before he licked his lips with that lustful look in his eyes. "You fixing everybody else problems but running from yo own. When you gone accept yo truth?"

"Trell, please, not now."

"Aiight um, I'mma go in da crib and let ya'll handle this." He looked at both of us knowing something was up but decided to give us some privacy instead.

I tried to walk away too but Trell grabbed me pulling me close to him. "You really tryna have this conversation right now with ya girl in the house? You trippin." I let him know.

"Man, you really wanna watch me be with somebody instead of just admitting yo feelings and telling LeLe she just gotta understand."

I dropped my eyes to avoid looking at him cause the way he was holding me had my pussy throbbing. "She thinks you gone dog me out Trell."

"But do you think I'mma dog you out?" He asked.

I thought about Liyah and how she was inside waiting for him. "Ion know what you will do, but I see how you doing ol girl you came here with cause you out here with me." I forced him to let me go. "And she's a damn fool cause I think you know not to try me like that. I'd be out here whooping yo ass."

I walked away leaving him to watch me. Inside, I was screaming to just say fuck it and be with him cause I was tired of running from my feelings. I just had to know he was truly ready. The more I thought about it, I completely understood LeLe's position in all of this. I would've felt the same way. At the same time, if she had some kind of security from us both I don't think it would've been such a big issue.

When I made it inside, George was talking to Mrs. Wells. "I'm glad everything is on one accord but I'm gonna tell you something hunny. Don't you ever get mad and refer to our son as a faggot again like you did a while back or else I'll leave you."

"Oh please George. I love my son and he knows it, even when I say fucked up shit but I'll never do that again." She told him before she addressed the guest. "Ya'll hungry? Ya'll better come on and eat cause when it's gone it gone! This a celebration! My boys are graduates!" She beamed while everyone clapped for the twins including myself.

I was glad to see at least something was finally coming together. I just wished my own life would come together. Preferably my love life. This shit sucked. A few minutes after I walked in, Trell came walking in. we locked eyes one more time before I walked to the kitchen to fix me a good old plate of southern foods. I didn't care how stressed this situation had me, I wasn't missing a meal.

Chapter 7

Leandra 'LeLe' Wells

I'd been busting my ass working nonstop since the graduation party and the only thing I could truly say I was happy about was the fact that my brothers had finally made up. I knew everything wouldn't be just perfect, but at least it was a start. I stood in the bathroom mirror looking at how exhausted I was. My sloppy bun was all over my head and I just looked so tired, on top of that my feet hurt so damn bad. Working these two jobs were kicking my ass but I had to keep in mind what I was doing it for. George and my mama didn't want me to pay any bills and neither did Trell since he tried to handle most of it. I still snuck and did it though and Trell cussed me the fuck out every single time. I still had an hour to go on my shift and I could leave and get some damn rest.

I didn't give a shit how many burgers or tacos these people needed. I was resting for the next two days since I'd taken off from both jobs. The only thing I had to do was see my probation officer and take a piss test. After that, I was gonna get my hair blown out, go get a mani and pedi, and then a damn massage. I felt so guilty about spending money on myself at times but Abbey was always stressing the importance of me having a pamper day to myself.

After splashing some water on my face and drying it, I was prepared to walk out when my phone ring with Karter's name flashing on the screen. I hadn't spoken to her since I found out the news about what her bitch ass sister had done to me. Matter of fact, I hadn't spoken to her ever since she sent me the picture of her little baby and that was months ago. I knew she thought I was avoiding her calls, but I wasn't. Truth was, I was just too busy to talk to her most of the time. She always called at the wrong damn time. "Hey." I answered.

"Well hey Queen." I haven't spoken to you in forever. "I swear I think you're dodging me and if so that's messed up cause I'm not my sister."

"Yeah, that was fucked up what she did to me but I'm not dodging you because of it." I assured her.

"I want you to know that I truly didn't know LeLe."

"I believe you, I know you didn't. It's okay. You don't need to be worried about this. You need to just keep focusing on taking care of that pretty baby."

"She's adorable. My whole heart." She beamed.

"Yeah, she is." I scratched my head and leaned up against the wall. "Why you hid the shit Karter? Who the fuck was gonna judge you?" I asked.

"Like I told everybody else, it was my own insecurities aiight? I'm always preaching. I know I look like a hypocrite."

"Kinda." I shrugged being totally honest with her. "But I mean, it's okay. It's your life."

"I guess." She replied. "I just wanted to check on you and assure you that I had nothing to do with that Kim situation. I'm so disappointed in her ya know? But I have to ask, what's your plans about it? That's still my sister."

"I'm not gonna do shit. Kim is suffering enough Karter. God is gonna handle her. That's why she's going through everything she's going through." I replied. The evil part of me wanted to kill her ass but killing her couldn't get my life back nor could it get my unborn child back, or Malik for that matter. Speaking of, I needed to really make it my business to at least see Majestic and his mama. "I'm on the clock so I gotta go Karter, I'll talk to you later."

"Okay Queen, I understand. Talk to you soon." She told me before we said our goodbyes and hung up. I had to take a deep breath before walking back out to the front. I hated this damn job and I especially hated my manager. I didn't know if he was obsessed with me or just really didn't like me cause he was always fucking with me and I didn't fuck with nobody. He looked like a old broke down peewee Herman in my book. As soon as I walked out he ask me to go take the garbage out to the back when he could've easily just took it himself, it wasn't even busy out front.

I didn't even fuss about it. I just grabbed the bags and walked out back to put the bags in the dumpster. As soon as I turned around I nearly shitted on myself when I saw the nigga standing behind me wearing a black hoodie. "What the fuck?!" I immediately started swinging and screaming when I felt him grab me. "What the fuck! Let me go!" He tried to stop me from swinging.

"Stop ma! It's me! It's Trey!" He growled in my ear removing his hoodie. "Don't fuckin' hit me again." He warned allowing me to see it was really him.

I don't know why, but I immediately started crying. "Where the fuck have you been Trey! I was so worried about you! Why the fuck you ain't tell me you was out!"

"Chill shorty! Chill." He pulled me in a bear hug. "I'm home, I'm out. I been out. I just had to lay low cause you know how the dicks play. They aint got shit on me but that don't mean they wont try to find shit. Stop crying."

"So what the fuck are you doing? You hiding now?" I asked wiping my eyes. "You could've at least told me you was home Trey?"

He looked agitated all of a sudden. "Did you hear anything I said?"

I looked over his shoulder. "Where's yo truck?"

"Got rid of that shit. I got me somethin' else. What time you get off?" He asked.

I looked down at my watch. "In a hour. Why?"

"We gone talk. I'mma wait for you."

"How did you even know where I worked Trey?" I asked.

"I'm always watchin'. You think I'mma leave you out here without knowing you good? I risked my own freedom for your shorty. That ain't no place for you."

I don't know what came over me but I hugged him again real tight. "Thank you so much! I can never repay you for that. I would've let them kill me first Trey."

My manager stuck his head out the door looking for me. "Leandra?" He asked confused.

Trey nod his head toward the building. "Go ahead. I'll see you when you get off."

I slowly walked away and then made it inside. My bitch ass manager didn't even want shit. He just wanted to get on my nerves. I decided to keep my mouth shut and just do my job without cussing his ass out and before I knew it, an hour had passed and I was off. When I walked out Trey was parked next to my car in a brand new truck, some kind of Infiniti truck. "Can you follow me to my house so I can at least park and get out of these clothes?" I asked when he rolled the window down. The deep scent of his cologne penetrated my nostrils smelling so good.

"I don't have all night shorty, I'll follow you but I'm not waiting for you to change and allat. My time is limited and I have moves to make." He let me know.

I knew he wasn't even the type of nigga to argue so I wasn't gonna argue with him. Besides, I was just happy he made it out. I thought I would never see his face again up until this point. "Okay, no problem."

I hopped in my car and drove home in silence just thinking. The way my spirit just gravitated towards Trey was crazy and vice versa. A part of me wanted to be so mad with him for not telling me he was back, but another part of me completely understood. As soon as I got home, I parked and then hopped in the car with Trey.

"I know I probably smell like some food. Sorry about that." I told him and then went to reach and turn his radio down. He gently slapped my hand away.

"What I tell you bout that?" He shook his head and then turned it down for me instead before he pulled off. "We just gone take a lil ride."

"My bad, I had to see if it was really you in there. I mean, you look the same but you've been gone so damn long." I teased. "I'm still so mad at you."

"You'll get over it. I'm was glad to know you made it out safe. I know that floor shit was uncomfortable but I had to do what I had to do." He let me know as he focused on the road.

"Is Cass out?" I asked.

"We ain't talkin' bout that nigga in here shorty. Don't look like he getting' out but if he do, I hope shit works out for him."

"What are your plans now?" I asked him.

He still had that serious look on his face. "I told you a long time ago ma. I'm my own man, I play by my own rules. I'm always prepared for a rainy day."

I slowly nod my head. "Um okay, that's good to know."

"I hope you got a plan. I mean, I see you got you another whip and workin' ya jobs and shit but all that's for nothing if you don't got a plan ma." He stopped at the red light and then just looked at me.

"What?" I asked.

"You women just don't fuckin' listen shorty. I went against the grain and gave you so many warnings to keep yo ass away. Too many warnings for my likings, you just wouldn't listen. What did you do with that bracelet?" He asked.

I almost asked him what bracelet he was talking about but I quickly remembered. He was talking about that charm bracelet Cass gave me. I had it in my jewelry box debating about what I wanted to do with it. "I have it put away. I might pawn it."

He shook his head. "Nah, no you wont. The dicks doin' sweeps on niggas and females too. You don't wanna draw that kinda attention to yourself. Go toss that bitch in the ocean somewhere or just never show it again. You lucky, real lucky. That shit violates yo probation even getting into the kind of relationship you was working yo way up to."

"Then what am I doing here with you Trey?"

"If you knew anything about me you'd know I'm cleaner than a whistle. I don't have a record. This the first time I've ever been arrested. I ain't never touched no dope and never would. I know how to play my cards ma. They can say what they want, they ain't got shit on me." He pulled his hoodie further back so I could see the mark on the side of his head. It was all healed up but I could tell it was a nasty one to begin with. "They wanted me to talk. I wouldn't so they beat my ass to try to make me. Ion even eat cheese ma, and I damn sho ain't no fuckin' rat."

I sighed again. "Like I said, I'm just glad you're out."

"Yeah well, me too." He told me rounding back around my corner. "I just hope you move smarter about the next nigga. Do ya research. You can't afford no petty ass mistakes."

"And what about CoCo?" I asked of his sister.

"Fuck CoCo." He replied. "She made her bed. Turned her back on me for that nigga when I tried to help her. CoCo is money hungry as fuck and that's all she cares about. When this shit clear up I'mma get my nephew and get the fuck outta Miami. I doubt CoCo getting out. Heard she about to take a plea for ten years."

"What?" My hands flew up to my mouth, I couldn't believe it. "What the fuck she do?"

"Everything. She did it all so fuck it."

"Well where's your nephew now?" I asked.

He just looked at me and shook his head once again. "Here you go with all the questions."

"I mean well shit; if you talk to me a little more I wouldn't have all of these questions. When you got locked up I realized I didn't know shit about you, not even your real name."

He simply nod his head and focused on the street.

"What do you expect Trey? Is that even your real name?"

"That's all you need to know."

"Listen." I said getting a little more agitated. "Where are your parents? I tried to go to CoCo's house and tell her to let your parents or whoever know that you got locked up but I couldn't because she was getting locked up too."

"My parents are fine, they don't need to be in the middle of my shit. I ever get locked up the only number you need is to my lawyer ma."

This was pointless. I exhaled loud as hell and just sat thinking while in front of the yard since we'd pulled back up. "I won't ask no more questions tonight." I told him.

"Thank God." Was his fucking reply. He got on my damn nerves some times. "You work tomorrow?"

"No."

"Aiight." He looked at the time on the dash. "I'll holla at you tomorrow."

I didn't say anything else. I just grabbed my purse and my house keys and got out the truck. Trey rolled down the window as soon as I stepped out. "Treyvon Carter."

"What?" I furrowed my brows.

"You wanted to know my real name right? That's the name ma. Treyvon Carter." He told me again and nod his head toward the house. "Go inside. Have a nice night ma." He slowly rolled the window back up and watched me walk inside the house. I repeated his name the entire time as I walked inside. Hell, I repeated his name even in the shower like a lil ass girl. Trey was the shit. I think I loved his ass. I don't know if it was because of the type of nigga he was, or because he help me from going to jail; all I knew was I felt something, even if I couldn't put my finger on it.

Chapter 8

Kimberly 'Kim' Laws

I thought working at working at Emily's law firm would be a piece of cake, but in reality it wasn't. This was one of the hardest jobs I ever had in my life but I didn't wanna fuck it up. I was almost finished with my program and the only time they let me out was to work. I was so glad this was my last week there. I was still undecided about where I wanted to go after, but Emily had already set me up with a cute little one bedroom space for me although I told her not to. She had already done way too much and I felt like I'd forever be in debt with her no matter how many times she expressed that she wanted nothing in return.

I felt so home sick. A part of me wanted to be back in Miami so badly, but it hurt every time I realized that I couldn't do that. That could only happen after I introduced Majestic to his child and prayed that he forgave me. If he didn't, at least I knew my baby would have a great family to raise him or her whenever I gave birth. I looked down at my stomach and sighed. Seemed like over night I swallowed a big ass pumpkin. My feet were always swollen and my back hurt so damn bad. I shook my damn head knowing I must've been high ass a damn kite when we made this baby. Had I been in my right state of mind I would've never kept having sex with Majestic unprotected knowing I'd get pregnant. Nobody couldn't pay me enough to do this shit all over again.

The mornings were the absolute fucking worst; just terrible. I couldn't make it out of the bed good before I was running to the toilet. Shit was strange cause I read online that a lot of women only deal with that the first three months. I was well into the seventh month and going through this now. I didn't go through any of this in the beginning cause if I did I would've had some kind of clue that I may have indeed been pregnant. My hat went off to all of the women who went through this shit cause I just couldn't even deal. It was hard enough trying to make it through the day as it is.

Paying attention to the ding on the clock I was happy as hell the clock read 5pm and it was time to go. I knocked on Emily's office door and waited for her to tell me to come inside. I only peeked my head in realizing she was on the line with a client. I silently mouthed to her and waved letting her know I was leaving. I rather had went to the little apartment she had set up for me but I had to finish this final week in my program. They even had a whole graduation and everything set up for us but I didn't wanna attend that part of it because I had nobody who would be there with me. Emily and Karter had already told me they couldn't make it for different reasons so I had to respect that. I knew if Abbey and LeLe were around and if shit was like it used to be, they wouldn't miss it for nothing. I hated that I fucked up so bad. If God could've granted me one wish, I would turn back the hands of time.

When I made it back to the facility, Lolita was sitting on my bed waiting for me. "Sup Lo, what you doing in here?" I asked tossing my stuff down. In the beginning they used to check my purse to make sure I didn't have shit in there but now, being so close to leaving those days were over with. Besides, they drug tested us on the regular and I always passed every single one with flying colors. She handed me a bag full of clothes. I opened it up and a huge smile spread across my face looking at all the unisex colored onsies and little outfits. "Aww you didn't have to do this. This is so nice of you."

"Yes I did cause yo ass ain't start buying shit yet so I sent Demarcus out to get some gifts from us both. Hope you like it."

"Whatever." I laughed. "Yeah, I love it. It's so damn cute." I took my time folding it back up. "I'mma start buying stuff soon. I have time."

She shook her head and chuckled. "You new mama's don't be knowing shit. At this point, that baby could come at any given time and you gotta be prepared."

"Yeah I guess you right." I told her thinking about it. I'd start getting stuff little by little. "You ready for graduation next week?"

"Yep, as ready as I'mma be. I'm ready to get back home. I feel it in my heart it's gone be better this time around."

"Good. Cause you got a good man girl." I told her.

Lolita's eyes smiled just thinking about him; I could tell. "Yeah, I guess I do." She made it to the door and turned around. "I'm going to sleep early girl. See you tomorrow." She told me. I watched Lo walk down the hall before closing the bag and stuffing it under my bed before I went to shower. I wanted to stay up and do a counseling session but I was too damn tired. Instead, I took my ass to sleep to so glad that I didn't have to eat anything. I'd eaten a big lunch today and because of that my fat ass was still full. Good!

~~~~~~~~

A week later there wasn't one dry face in the room after we graduated and said our goodbyes and well wishes to each other. Lo was reunited with her family and after we made a promise to keep up with each other, she left. Tossing my bags in my trunk; I went to make sure that I said goodbye again to Mrs. Andrews cause she was a big help while I was here and helped me cope with a lot in the beginning. She was like a mother figure to us all in here. "You make sure you take care of that little angel." She rubbed my belly with a smile.

"Will do." I assured her.

"And make sure ya'll come see me."

"I'll make sure we do that too."

"Please do." She hugged me again. "Now run along girl. Go get your life back. I don't want to catch you at a place like this again. You gotta learn to be stronger than life or it'll beat you up every single time."

"Thank you Mrs. Andrews. I'll remember that." I told her.

When I got to the car, I put my new address in the GPS and drove there. I'd seen it before it. Finding it was the only problem since I wasn't from around here. If this was back in Miami, I'd know it with my eyes closed. I finally made it after fighting traffic for damn near an hour. I didn't bring my bags in though. Shit, my damn back was killing me so I decided I would come back out later to get them out of the trunk. I had a few things in my dresser drawers and closets anyway; at least everything that I would need. I put the keys on the counter, took my shoes off and flopped on the couch wishing I had a man that could rub my feet for me. It felt good to let them breath although I hated the appearance. Looked like little pigs feet as swollen as my toes were.

Finally finding the energy after damn near an hour or so; I took a shower and made myself comfortable before making me a salad. Emily and Karter had my fridge and my freezer stacked. I wouldn't have to shop for a good little while and my rent was even paid off for the first 3 months. After I finished the homemade Caesars salad, I laid down on the couch watching the first season of 'Stranger Things' with a big blanket over me trying to ignore the stabbing from the sharp pains I was feeling in my side and in my lower abdomen. I figured I had some kind of gas or something so I kept massaging it and changing the position I was laying in. When that didn't work, I made me a hot cup of tea. It kinda worked a little bit, I mean, it made me sleepy. I called Karter before I could fall asleep though and explained to her what I was feeling.

"You're portably fine Kim. Probably your uterus just stretching or gas. Maybe you just need to get some rest."

I yawned all prepared to stop fighting my sleep. I did need to rest. "Okay you know what? You're probably right. I'll see how I'm feeling when I wake up." I told her. I don't even think I hung up the phone good before my eyes met the back of my eyelids. I didn't know how long I slept either but when I woke up, it was dark outside. Standing up from the couch, I still felt the pain just not as bad and the only thing that made me content was the fact that I could still feel my little baby moving. I took drunk a cold bottle of water and then took another hot shower. This time when I laid down it was in my big comfy bed.

The next morning when I woke up, the sun was shining through the blinds in my room. Feeling the strong urge to pee, I hopped up wearing only my panties and a T-shirt to run to the bathroom when I felt something in my coochie that I would say felt like a little pop before warm fluid was trickling down the inside of my thighs. The tears were coming right after cause I knew my water broke and it was way too soon. "Calm down Kim, calm down." I coached myself. I didn't have shit for this baby, I didn't even have a bassinet or nothing. I wasn't prepared for this at all but that was the least of my worries. At seven months, I knew it was way too soon; I just prayed that my baby would be okay. Instead of calling Emily and Karter, I called the damn ambulance cause I damn sho wasn't driving myself risking this baby slipping right outta my pussy in the drivers sear. Hell no, not me.

The contractions came shortly after but I sat on the couch taking deep breaths after the paramedics arrived to take me away. They asked me so many times on the way there about if I had family I needed to call. How many weeks was I. Was this my first child, all kinda shit that I just couldn't think right now to be answering all these damn questions right now. Only thing I could think of was to try to stay calm and breath so that's what I did with my eyes closed until we arrived.

They put me in a room bypassing observation since my water was completely ruptured. I couldn't believe this was it. I had so many mixed feelings about this day. They actually did everything to try to prevent me from delivering early but nothing was working to stop this labor. This little baby decided that this was the time. I didn't have a choice besides to do this alone and I must admit, this was one of the most fucked up feelings in the world. I made this bed and I had to lay in it. I always thought if I ever had a kid I would be surrounded by love and as a family or something. Maybe a husband or a man who loved me along side of me telling me it would be okay. Instead, I was surrounded by doctors and nurses that I didn't even know in excruciating pain getting ready to push a baby out of my ass. Upon arrival I was already six centimeters dilated, there was simply nothing they could do.

By the time Emily arrived in a panic, my baby's head was already out and I was screaming from the pain feeling like everything had been ripped right out of my body. I had begged, and fussed, and cussed to get an epidural but because how far along dilated I was they couldn't give it to me. I had to thug it out and this was by far the absolute worst pain I'd ever felt in my life. This shit hurt more than my stepfather ripping through my little 12 year old vagina taking my virginity and popping my cherry.

"It's a boyyyy!" The nurses beamed knowing I didn't know the sex. Emily's face was flushed red. She ran out of here as fast as she walked in when she saw all of the blood and childbirth up close and personal. I was happy but exhausted as hell and could barely keep my eyes open. They didn't allow me to hold him yet. As soon as he came busting out, they allowed me to glance at him and they took him. He looked like a little pink baby doll with a head full of hair and he was super tiny.

"Is he okay?" I asked crying like a baby hoping he was okay. I couldn't see what they were doing to him but I did hear his little cries.

"Baby is strong mom." One of the nurses assured me. "He's four pounds and fourteen inches long." She told me before they allowed me to hold him for a few minutes after. I couldn't believe how much he looked mike Majestic and Malik. It was so scary because he looked more like Malik than Majestic. I burst into tears. God was really punishing me in the worst way. He wasn't going to let me forget none of the shit I'd done.

Emily stroked my hair and consoled me. "It's okay Kim. He just looks funny right now but he will grow into his looks." She said being dead serious. "They all look like hamsters at first."

I didn't know if I was still crying or crying and laughing at the same damn time. I didn't think anything was wrong with my baby. He was so adorable to me. The nurses came to take him away to run test on him since he's technically considered a premature baby. Although only four pounds, his lungs could be very immature. I just prayed that everything would be okay. "I can't believe I'm a mom." I cried.

"You'll be a great mom." Emily said.

If only she knew the truth. I didn't know how long I had to even be a mom. When it was all said and done and Emily had gone it was just me in this cold room left to stare at these walls. My baby had to go to the NICU because just like they predicted, his lungs weren't strong enough so he just needed a little extra help. I picked up my cell phone and fumbled around with it contemplating on making the call. It only too me a few seconds before I did. I called Majestic's phone blocked. When he actually picked up my heart dropped and my voice box froze. I couldn't say anything, I guess I wasn't ready. I hung up and sat the phone on the bed next to me.

The nurse came in a little bit after to press down on my stomach to prevent me from getting blood clots I guess. She also gave me an pain pill to help me cope with the pain. Next she gave me something to help me relax and get some rest. Before I knew it, I was out again sleeping like a baby. A part of me should've been happy but I couldn't ignore that little voice in my head that was telling me to count my days.

Chapter 9

Leon Wells

"You didn't have to do all of this." Kevin beamed looking at the setup I had prepared for him. I know he thought I set all this shit up in my living room for us to have a private dinner with a chef and everything but I didn't. This was all on LeLe. I had her ass up early getting everything setup. I let her pick out our menu for tonight and everything. I just wanted to show Kevin that I meant what I said. We'd been getting along good so far since I came out the closet. He'd even introduced me to his family. I was still kinda hesitant about bringing him around mine. I wasn't tryna push it so I was taking baby steps when it came to that. "This is so nice."

"I'm glad you like it." I told him. I didn't have to pull out the chair for Kevin to sit down and all that other shit that a man had to do for a woman. We weren't like that. We both were still men at the end of the day, we didn't look all flamboyant and shit. We dressed how we wanted and we did what we wanted. I had some good news too. I'd gotten the job offer to work in the Forensics Department with the Broward Sheriff's Office making some good money. I still hadn't told Kevin yet. He had just got accepted into Law School so I wanted him to have his moment. "I was up in here working all day to get this shit right."

As soon as I said that I heard a loud thud from the back before LeLe walked out with her purse getting ready to leave. "Oh no the fuck you didn't." She sassed. She then spoke to Kevin. "Hey Kevin, glad you could make it but you know damn well Leon didn't do no sit like this. It was his idea but I'm the one that made it all come together." She then smiled knowing damn well she wasn't supposed to rat me out.

"Go grab a piece of cheese while you at it." I told her.

She shot me the middle finger. "Fuck you."

Kevin laughed. "Ya'll are so cute. It's fine, I appreciate it either way."

"Well, you have the personal chef all to yourself so eat up as much as you can. I'm out. Catch ya'll later." She yelled behind her as she walked out of the door.

"Soooo." Kevin picked up the menu. "What are we eating?"

"You can have whatever you like."

"In that case I'll have a steak cooked well done with some loaded mashed potatoes and asparagus. I need a salad on the side and some bread rolls too."

"Sounds good. I think I'mma fuck with that too." I told him looking at my watch.

"You know this is the third time you've checked that watch since I've been here. Is everything okay? We got somewhere to go?" Kevin asked.

I didn't realize I was clock watching but truth was, I was waiting for Trell to come. He was supposed to be here over thirty minutes ago. This would've been a good time for Kevin and him to squash that beef but after a hour passed I figured he wasn't coming. Kevin didn't let up. "So you wanna tell me or no?" He asked dabbing his mouth with a napkin after munching down on his steak.

"To be honest I was waiting for Trell. He knew you would be here but he didn't show up. I mean, I guess it's gone take more time." I would be lying if I said I didn't feel a way. I would've done this for him without a doubt.

Kevin reached over the table and grabbed both of my hands into his. "Listen, things like this can't be forced babe. It has to fall in place on it's own time. You've done enough so far and that's good enough with me. Trust me, he will come around."

I was getting ready to agree with him but was distracted by the knocking on the door. I made sure I had my gun in the small of my back before I went and opened it. It was Trell, he walked in looking bothered as fuck though. He clapped me up before walking in. "I don't know if I'm just paranoid or what but a nigga feel like I been getting followed all fuckin' day long."

I peeked my head out the door. I didn't see shit that looked unusual. I walked to the blinds and looked from the window next and still didn't see shit. "Nah you probably just paranoid bro. I don't see shit." I closed the blinds back.

"You probably right." He said taking a piece of bread from the table. He then took a look at Kevin.

I knew Kevin didn't even wanna give it a chance to get awkward so he stood up from his chair and extended his hand to Trell's. "I wanna apologize about hitting you that day man. That was truly my bad and I had no business doing that. I'd like to start over if you don't mind. My name is Kevin."

Trell looked from Kevin's hand back to the bread he was holding in his own hand. He decided to finish the bread first and the shook his hand real quick. "I appreciate that Kevin, but I'm not apologizing for defending myself. Shit you swung on me so I had to handle up. We past that though."

"I can take that." Kevin replied. "Just glad we can be right here right now. This is pretty big."

Trell just simply nod his head. "So what's this? Ya'll had a lil dinner date?" He asked grabbing a piece of asparagus from my plate that I didn't eat and popped it in his mouth. He took a seat at the table and stared at us both. "So how does this work, like who the man and who the woman. Who wears the pants in this shit?"

Kevin looked like he didn't know what to say but I knew Trell well enough to know he was playing cause that's not some shit he would really wanna know. Kevin's face turned beet read. "Umm yeah so this is awkward." He said.

I chuckled. "Trell... nigga..."

Trell shook his head and frowned. "You know goddamn well ion wanna know some shit like that. I just wanted to fuck with ya'll a lil bit." He shrugged. "You know, cause if ya'll gone be all out in the open and shit with this relationship then ya'll better have some tough ass skin cause muhfuckas is wicked."

"I'm not worried bout nobody fuckin' with me." I assured Trell.

"I'll kill they ass." He said in all seriousness. Meanwhile, Kevin looked back and forth from us both. Trell stood up to leave. "I didn't wanna stay too long and interrupt ya'll little steak dinner and shit. I'mma head on out and make some rounds."

"Where you goin'?" I asked.

"Nigga mind ya business."

I looked at him like he was crazy. I never did get a chance to holla at him about him and Abbey. "Wussup with you and Abbey nigga? What's that shit all about?"

"Damn." He mumbled. "Every time I try not to think about this fucking girl her fucking name come up now I'mma be thinking bout her ass all night. If she know like I know she better jump on this ride cause a nigga getting drafted. I'm claiming that. Ion give a fuck if it's not the first round picks, it's happening."

"So what's the problem?" I asked.

"Man she worried about LeLe cause LeLe don't want us fuckin' around. She think I'mma dog her friend out."

"Well are you?" Kevin asked. "I'm sorry, I'm just curious."

"Nah, not her." Trell replied before grabbing his keys. "Fuck you had to bring her up? Damn." He said again. Just by the way he was acting I knew he was probably gone end up over there.

"Ya'll better stop playin' nigga. You slip somebody else gone grip."

"Shit, tell her that. I been preaching this shit for the longest but then when she see me come around with Liyah she wanna trip. I see the way she be side eyeing a nigga and shit."

"I noticed." I told him. "Well you go handle that. We got a movie to catch."

We clapped it up again before he walked out. I peeped how he pulled out his gun when he walked to the car. Trell must've been serious about feeling like he was being followed cause he wasn't no paranoid ass nigga and he never showed his gun unless he was planning on using it.

"Is everything okay?" Kevin asked.

"Hold up, I'll be right back." I adjusted my own gun and walked out to the parking lot trying to catch Trell. He was already gone though. When I got back inside I called his phone. It was something about that twins intuition shit. I didn't feel right now. He had me worried. "Yo?" He picked on the first ring.

"You sure you good?" I asked him.

"Yeah, I'm aiight. I'mma go holla at Abbey, fuck it." He said.

"Send me a text and let me know when you made it. Shit, you got me paranoid now."

"I'mma be aiight. I got you." He told me before hanging up.

After that, Kevin helped me clean up after I tipped the chef and sent her on her way. I didn't feel like going to the movies no more cause Trell had my fucking brain fried right now and I hated worrying and shit. However, I didn't want Kevin to think I was back on my bullshit trying to hide him and shit so we went anyway. My body was in the theater when we got there but my mind was somewhere else. Only thing brought me a lil relief was the fact that Trell text me and let me know when he made it. It took everything in me, but I decided to focus on the movie and make sure Kevin had my undivided attention. Even if it was just for a few minutes.

Chapter 10

Abbey Daniels

"Fuck no Trell." I tried to push him away from my door. "You don't have that right to just be popping up around here like this no more. What if I had company?"

Trell wasn't trying to hear shit I had to say as he forced his way in anyway. "Shut the fuck up and kiss me."

"What?" I sassed with one hand on my hip.

"You know you want to." He walked up on me smelling like weed with a mixture of his cologne.

"Boy please. I'm over that shit."

"You never did lie too good." He forcefully placed his lips on top of mine arousing a kiss out of me; a deep passionate kiss too. If I wasn't on my cycle I would've jumped all over his dick. Just like sugar, I melted to his touch and for that I was cussing my own ass out. At this point it wasn't even about LeLe, this shit was deeper than rap. It's just the simple fact that he really thought it was okay to keep flaunting Liyah in my face and at this point I was almost sure he was doing that shit on purpose.

In the beginning, I had so much control but now I didn't like how his young ass had turned me the fuck out and had me feeling a way. At the same damn time he could try to front all he wanted. Liyah was pretty and all but she wasn't no Abbey. He knew that lil bitch couldn't do it like me. Trell grabbed a handful of my ass. I felt his hard dick pressed up against me and I had to stop him. It never failed how we were like two dogs in heat all the fucking time when we were alone with each other. "Don't start no shit Trell." I gasped in between kisses. "My period is on and ion let no niggas run red lights on me."

He snatched back and looked at me when he caught on to what I was saying. "Come on man, that shit nasty as fuck." Trell looked disgusted. "Anyway why you think I only come around to fuck you? Is that the only thing you think I care about? I be comin' to chill, that be yo lil freak ass on the other shit."

I used my pointer finger and mushed him in the forehead. "Boy, I know you fuckin' lyin'." I chuckled.

"You know you miss me. Ion even know why you be actin' like that."

"Where's Liyah?" I quizzed.

"Why you asking bout her? I'm here with you ain't I?"

"The question is, does she know that?" I asked in all seriousness.

"It ain't her business."

"Yeah aiight." I flopped down on the couch flipping through the channels.

"Where the fuck Kim at?" He asked out the blue. "I ain't seen her in a minute."

"We ain't fucking with Kim right now." I told him not wanting to say too much more about it. LeLe would talk about it when she was ready, it wasn't my place.

He shook his head. "Female shit." He replied. "Get up and throw on something." He ordered.

"Un Un." I shook my head. "I'm not finna play with you cause I gotta work in the morning." I told him.

"I'll back early. Just slip on something." He told me again. Knowing Trell he wasn't gonna let it go so it didn't hurt to get out for a few. I put on a comfortable Juicy Couture suit with some white Nikes. I sprayed on a little body spray and grabbed my cute little Chanel bag before going outside hopping in his passenger seat. "Roll this for me." He told me passing some wrap with a little weed bag that he'd already broken down. I did as I was told and licked on the grape flavored Dutch wrap until the joint was perfect. I didn't light it up though cause that was too risky if we got pulled over for any reason.

He didn't tell me where we were going and I didn't ask. With the music loud as hell we both just vibe out deep in our own thoughts until we reached Hallandale Beach. "This where you wanted to go?" I asked getting out with him.

"Shit, sometime it's good to get away from everything and everybody and just think for a minute. When everything around you moving so fucking fast, it's impossible to just think. Light up the blunt." He told me when we made it to the sand. It was so peaceful out here listening to the sounds of the waves crashing against each other. I passed it to him and he took a pull before we went back and forth with it.

We were both sitting down but Trell allowed he to sit in between his legs with my back pressed up against his chest. "So peaceful. I need to do this more often." I told him feeling high as a kite already. I felt damn good. "Between my patients and our crazy ass worlds, I need a good peaceful situation like this some times."

"Yeah I hear you." He said.

"What's up with you?"

"Nothin' ma, just tired of asking you what you wanna do. I'm just tryna figure out if you ridin' or what? I'm ready to give up on yo ass."

"I would hate that." I told him truthfully. "To be honest Trell, I don't wanna have to fuck you up and I'd hate to ruin the friendship part of us by getting in a relationship all because you think you want one thing and then when I give you that you figure out that you don't. Like, it's no rush. You got time to play with them hoes, but I'm not giving you multiple times to play with me."

"Respect a grown ass man when he talking to you ma. If I didn't know what I wanted I wouldn't even be here right now. Had you been any other female I would've been gave up on yo ass. I ain't never did shit to make you doubt me before so ion know why you doin' that shit now. To be honest, this my last night doin' this shit with you. That's why I brought you here. No distractions, nobody else around, just us."

I knew I fucked with Trell about his age a lot but to be honest, he was realer and way more mature than a lot of niggas I knew. I can truthfully say he ain't never lied to me and always kept it a buck even if it's some shit I didn't agree with. I thought about everybody else around me who was doing whatever to make themselves happy. I felt like I deserved that same happiness. If they could have happiness, why couldn't I? I don't think it was one person walking this earth who could say they could help who they loved. I know I couldn't and God knows I tried.

I simply nod my head and smiled. No more doubts or wondering, if Trell was sure this is what he wanted than I was down. We would have to just make LeLe understand. "Okay Trell, we can try this shit but I'm telling you now if it don't work I'm not trying again. I'm giving you time to clear up yo loose ends and I'll do the same on my end but if we gone do this than lets do it."

"You mean it right? This ain't no emotional ass shit and ya period just talkin' or no shit like that?"

I playfully turned around and mushed him in the head while laughing. "Stop playing with me Trell."

"Yo what I told you about that shit?" He gave me that side way look. "I'mma fuck you up one of these days." He warned me before asking for a kiss.

I placed my lips up against his kissing him long and hard. Deep down inside, I was scared to fully give Trell all of me but it was fair to both of us to at least try. We would never know what could've been if we both just walked away. When it was time for us to leave the beach we went back to my house and Trell decided he would stay. Some times the best nights were when a man just held on to you and made you feel secure. Sex could never beat a bond. Yes, the sex was good. Matter of fact it was great, but in reality you couldn't just lay up with everybody cause it was all about the sex.

"I love you." He told me before we both dozed off.

"I love you too." I assured him. "Please don't make me regret this Trell."

"Nah you won't. I got you." He kissed my forehead. "Go to sleep."

With that, I was out.

Chapter 12

Abbey Daniels

The next morning, Trell had to go and I needed to talk to LeLe so I called her. "Morning. Rise and Shine." I sang happily in the phone.

"What the hell you so happy about? Morning." She yawned.

"You have work today?" I asked her.

"I did but I'm calling out cause my body is too tired."

"Great, get dressed. I'm coming to get you. We need to talk."

She sucked her teeth. "About what? Must be Trell cause why else do you have to take me away to talk? Furthermore, what else could you possibly wanna talk about?"

"Actually, yes it is about Trell so do you wanna hear it or not?"

"Come on, I'm ready for your ass." She hung up in my face. I called Trell after.

"Morning Beautiful." His deep voice boomed through the phone bringing music to my ears.

I blurted it out. "I'mma tell LeLe about us today. Right now; I'm about to head over there and she's just gone have to listen to what I have to say."

Trell chuckled. "I been lookin' for them balls forever. It's about time they finally grew cause if you think LeLe ain't gone be happy with who she wanna be happy with you must be outta your mind."

"I know, I know." I giggled. "I'll call you later." I assured him.

I grabbed my keys and flew out of the house. I made it to LeLe in less than 30 minutes and George let me in the house. "Good morning George." I spoke.

"Morning Abbey." He step to the side and let me in. "Leandra is in the back."

When I got to LeLe's room and opened the door she was sitting on the edge of her bed wrapped up in a towel putting lotion on her legs. "Close the door back." She told me without stopping what she was doing.

I closed the door and then locked it too before sitting my purse on her dresser with my keys. This bitch had been to prison around some of the toughest women in the world. If she attacked me, my ass needed to be ready cause I wasn't so sure I could beat her in a one-on-one. Her ass probably learned all kinda shit on the yard. "Listen LeLe, ain't no other way to say this shit ok? I love Trell and he loves me too. We was both wrong for hiding shit from you and maybe we shouldn't have even started fucking around in the first place but it happened and now this is where we at."

She was still giving me a serious look. "Okay, so get to the point."

"What you mean? That's what I'm doing. We decided we're gonna be together and if it works it works, if it doesn't than it doesn't but at least we know we tried. We promise not to involve you. That was agreed on both ends."

She just simply shook her head and sucked her teeth. "You it shouldn't have ever happened, but ion have nothing else to say about it. Ya'll are grown you can do what you want but just don't come telling me shit if it goes left cause I'm not turning on my brother."

I could tell she really didn't like this and yes, I could clearly see her concerns of this putting her in a fucked up spot but we gotta do what we gotta do. I didn't have much else to say cause her seriousness was making me nervous so I pulled the George card. "When we were coming up and you decided that you would be the one to take all the boys lunch money and then we used it to by all kinda ice cream and shit, did I judge you? Did I judge you when…"

LeLe raised one finger and cut me off laughing. "Hold up bitch, if you think you bout to stand here and pull a George on me you must be outta yo damn mind. You will not."

"I'm just saying." I shrugged.

"Just saying my ass. Fuck that. I said I get it."

"Well good." I told her removing the small can of mace from out of my bra placing it back inside of my purse. "Cause I thought you were gonna try to attack me and I was gonna have to mace your ass. I'm not fighting no bitch that came off the yard. Ya'll don't fight regular like us regular bitches on the street. Ya'll fight in survival mode and shit."

"Whatever Abbey." She rolled her eyes and then slipped on a pair of Nike tights with the matching sports bra and the matching shoes. She had her hair blown out so she took the wrap off and combed her hair down as it flowed right above her bra strap looking all silky and shit. "Where we going?"

"Ion know, I guess to get some breakfast." I told her.

"Sounds good." She told me while grabbing her stuff to head out. She looked like something was on her mind. She spoke what was on her mind before we even made it to the door. "Have you seen Majestic?" She asked. "I really been wanting to talk to him."

"I haven't seen that nigga but to be honest Kim's bitch ass needs to come back and be here to tell him. Who's to say he's gone believe it coming from either one of our mouths? Kim done disappeared and for all he knows you could just be pulling some punk as shit. How convenient to throe it off on a person who not even around to confirm if that's true or not?"

There was a little silent pause and I could tell she was really letting that sink in. "You right. Ion wanna make shit worst than what it is. While everybody making shit right I would've loved to do the same."

"I know. Your time will come."

As soon as we walked outside, the sun kissed both of our faces causing us to use our hands as a shield. We didn't even make it to my car when an Infiniti truck pulled up. The window rolled down and Trey was behind the driver seat. "Trey?" I asked all excited. "What the hell? It's like you came back from the dead or something." I said too happy to see his face. I was wondering why LeLe was acting like it was nothing.

"Wussup ma." He casually spoke to me and then looked at LeLe. "Where yo clothes at shorty?"

LeLe looked herself up and down. "I'm wearing them. What's up Trey?" She asked with a lustful look in her eyes.

Oh hell naw. I thought to myself. This bitch been hiding shit. She wasn't even shocked to see this man or nothing. "Am I missing something here?"

"No." She laughed at me. "I forgot he was coming to pick me up this morning Abbey." She looked at me sincere. "Don't be mad, we can catch up later today." She said.

"Wait a minute. So you knew Trey was home? You didn't even tell me."

"I forgot." She shrugged walking to his car to get in the passenger seat. "By the way Abbey. Trey is home." She sang with this smile on her face before getting in the car closing the door. Trey nod his head at me before rolling up the window and pulling off. The smile on my face was plastered. I know Trey was a different kind of thug but I hope LeLe ended up with him. Ion know what it was about him but I liked him for her. I knew he wasn't a bitch like Cass.

I wasn't even mad that she bounced with the nigga. Most bitches can't even get close to Trey so I would've done the same fucking thing. I called Trell when I got back in the car to ask him if he wanted to hang out but he didn't answer either. I figured he was somewhere training or tying up some of his lose ends. I'd give him time to call me back but since I had some time off, I was going to pamper myself.

Chapter 13

Leandra 'LeLe' Wells

I sunk down into Trey's soft leather seats and decided to wait until we pulled off to speak. "Morning Trey."

"Morning shorty." He replied adjusting the visor in front of him to keep the sun out of his face.

"So where are you taking me? What was so important today?" I asked. Since Trey got back in town it seemed like we spoke every day and everyday he opened up to more just a little more. He went from being quiet and cold to quiet and warm. I think he was still trying to figure me out but had he been paying attention, which I'm sure he was then he would see that.

"It's a surprise. Just thought I'd give you a lil more motivation. I ran into somebody I used to know and just so happened they were tryna get somebody to buy out their restaurant space for a little of nothin' cause they just tryna get out the business. I figured you could look at it. May need to install some grease traps and shit if they don't have none but I saw it. It's in decent shape. You shouldn't need much capitol. I got people who can come clean it up for you and shit." He informed me still focusing on the road.

"Trey you foreal?" I asked with a huge smile on my face.

"Yeah shorty. Ion want you getting' too comfortable. I'm sure you got the bread and whatever you don't have I might match you, but I think you can do this on yo own. You just doubtin' yo' self."

"I think I can too. I've been busting my ass working two jobs and saving adding on to what I already had. It ain't easy."

"I came from da trenches. I know how that shit go. I'm not no spoon fed nigga so I get it." He said nodding his head.

We pulled up in front of a plaza on 183rd and 441 where the place was located. I stepped out into the scorching heat again and I felt my hair frizzing up already. I just knew my shit was about to be too threw that's why I had a hair tie with me just in case I needed to throw this shit right back on top of my head into a bun like I always did. Trey had the key to get inside and he was right. As soon as I stepped in, I had a vision. I closed my eyes and imagined how I would want the place to look. When I opened my eyes Trey was staring at me with those deep browns of his surrounded by those thick lashes and bushy brows. "You like it?" He asked.

I nod my head. "I do, I just need to see the kitchen." He led me to the back where the kitchen was and I just fell in love. It was the perfect size for me and a small staff. "How much does he want?" I asked.

"He wants fifteen for this space. You'll need bout ten to fifteen more if the spot need a grease trap remodel or some more equipment." He said calmly while talking to me and doing numbers on his phone. "I mean, ion really know how this shit go, having a restaurant ain't my dream. I'm just here to help."

"Okay I think I should set up to have an inspector come and look at it first and then after that we can go from there. If everything is everything then I'll buy it and get started. I'm not quitting my jobs right now though."

"Nah, you ain't suppose to. You gotta keep using that to finance yo dreams until ya spot ready. I knew you had a lot of brains in there somewhere." He told me smiling. I couldn't believe it. This nigga never ever smiled.

"I can't believe you just did that?" I cheesed.

"What?"

"Smiled." I told him.

"Ion do that shit for everybody."

"But you did it for me though." I told him still walking around checking stuff out.

Trey didn't say anything else. He just watched me do my thing while he shot the man a text. "You got an inspector you know?"

I shook my head. "Nope but I can find one."

"Don't worry bout that. I got one. He just text and said he was gone be here next week Wednesday a lil after noon. If you can't make it I'll meet him here."

"Good." I said. "I'll be here for sure and I still want you here."

"I can do that." He assured me.

When we made it back to the truck Trey turned the music down since he knew I was gonna do it anyway. I always had a question. "So what you doing with yourself Trey?"

"I'm good ma. I own a few properties. I've always invested my money. While niggas was buying a bunch of irrelevant shit and being flashy and shit I was purchasing properties. I own a few homes and two duplexes. I invested in stocks and shit. Some shit the black community is rarely educated about. I'm good, trust me. I really wanna build a private apartment complex with about fifty to sixty units and only rent them out to single mothers with low income. Some shit to help them get on they feet. The first year I'd let them live rent free. If they don't have they shit together within that year then they on they own. Ion know what to tell'em."

"Oh my God. I think that is so dope Trey. Like foreal."

"Yeah, that's what I been workin' on lately. Tryna see if I can get it done. When I conquer what I wanna conquer here; I'm headed to Atlanta to do the same shit."

It made me nervous hearing him say he was going to Atlanta. Like what about me? Was this about to be a situation with us or was he keeping this platonic? I didn't understand but I didn't wanna push it. I could tell he's the type of nigga that didn't easily just jump into things. He had to check the temperature first. At the same time, I was smart enough to know he was getting some pussy from somewhere cause if a nigga didn't do nothing else; he was gone do that.

"You know what else would be dope?" I asked.

"What?"

"Would you rent that place out to mothers just coming home from prison as well? Like would a record stop them from being accepted? I'm asking cause this has to be one of the hardest things ever. Like society wants us to do better but yet when we try to do better they try to hold us back. If we put our conviction on a rental application we get denied. We're limited on the jobs we can have because of the same thing." I shared with him. This wasn't just a problem for the black community. This was a problem for anybody who had ever been to prison and wanted to make a change.

"I would definitely do that." He said like he was thinking about it as he stroked his goatee.

"I think you should." I replied.

He continued to focus on the road. I didn't know where our next stop was but I was enjoying his company like I always did. "What do you read? What Kinda music you like?" He asked catching me off guard. Nobody had ever asked me no shit like this.

"I like a lot of music and books." I replied.

He furrowed his brows like my response frustrated him. "See, it's answers like that. That shit blows me with woman ma. They be complaining when niggas don't try to get to know them in that way but when we do we get basic answers like that. Tell me, give me a little detail." He said. "Me personally, I like all kinda music. Old school and rap is my thing though. I like Kevin Gates, T.I., Nipsey Hussle,

Jeezy, and Tupac. That's just to name a few. I like rap niggas who spitting some real knowledge in they raps; that intellectual shit. The old school part of the music is just cause its good music. That old shit had a meaning to it. When dudes like Luther Vandross, Frankie Beverly, Rick James, Barry White play on the radio you can feel that shit in ya soul. Them niggas sang from the heart. That's the type of music that made families come together and have a good time." He said spitting some knowledge. I only knew who a few of those people were. "As far as books, I've read some pretty dope shit. I'll read anything that feeds my brain. It can't be no bullshit."

"Yeah, I'm not a huge fan of old school but I'll listen to it cause being in prison, I learned how to adapt to all music. I'll even listen to country music and rock for that matter. I'm a chameleon when it comes to that but before I went in I would've never listened to none of that shit. I love books though, that's how most of my days passed me by faster by reading and feeding my brain. I've read 'Blood In My Eye' by George Jackson. I've read 'Contagious' by Jonah Berger." I told him. "Oh!" I snapped my fingers. "I've read 'Message To The Black Man In America' by Elijah Muhammad. You should read that one. It's so good."

"I'm actually impressed ma. That's wussup. I'mma make sure I grab those." He said.

"Yeah you should." I told him. "I like urban fiction too though. That shit takes us women to a whole different world."

"Yeah I heard." He chuckled.

Next we stopped in the hood to get something to eat from Shuckin & Jivin. Trey and me had some good conversation. We had learned so much about each other in less than 24 hours and when it was time for him to drop me back off, it was well after the evening and I wasn't ready to go at all but I would never tell him that. "Thanks for a good day Trey. I really enjoyed myself."

"No problem ma." He simply nod his head and gave me a half smile. I knew he was watching me walk inside cause he didn't pull off until I made it inside. I didn't know where my mama and George were but they weren't home so I peeled my outfit off and took a shower since that sun had done some damage today. I felt so sticky, and exhausted might I add. As soon as I made it to my room I lay across the bed replaying Trey's and me conversation. He was definitely different. I can't remember not one person ever getting that deep with me wanting to know the specifics about everything that I liked until now.

Before I went to bed, I pulled out my notepad and started scribbling my own little blueprint and a list of everything I would need for a restaurant. I knew the colors I wanted it and everything. I knew the kind of tables and chairs I wanted and all. I would come up with a whole menu soon as well. I was so excited I could hardly contain myself. I knew this process wouldn't happen over night because greatness took time but I was willing to put in the work to do what I needed to do. Eventually, I burned myself out and fell asleep only to be awaken in the middle of the night by Abbey. "Hey girl didn't mean to wake you." She said.

I didn't even open my eyes as I spoke. "What's wrong?"

"Have you spoken to Trell?" She asked.

I sucked my teeth so fucking hard. "See, this the shit I'm talking about. Ya'll starting this bullshit already." I told her beyond irritated now.

"No it ain't like that LeLe, seriously this is more of a worried type of call. I haven't seen him since this morning nor have I spoken to him. I just feel like something might be wrong. I just wanna make sure he's okay. Seriously."

"I'll call Leon and see if he's heard from him. I'll tell you what though. If he is with a bitch somewhere then don't say I didn't try to warn you."

"Nah ion even think that LeLe. If that is the case though. I'll let you have that. Just call Leon and let me know."

"Aiight." I told her before hanging up and immediately dialing Trell's number and getting no answer. I called Leon next. I called him twice and he didn't pick up so I called Kevin hoping that he was with him. "Hey Kevin sorry to wake you. This is LeLe."

"I know." He replied sounding still asleep. "Are you okay?"

"Actually I'm looking for Leon, are ya'll together?" I asked.

"Yeah let me wake him up." I heard shuffling in the background. "Babe... your sister is on the phone."

A few seconds later Leon was on the line. "Sup LeLe? Everything okay?"

"Have you spoken to Trell?" I asked.

"No not today. Why what happen?" He asked. "I could tell he was awake now cause he didn't sound sleep anymore.

"Abbey seems to think something is wrong cause he's been missing all day. I called him and he didn't answer either."

Silence.

"Leon?"

"Yeah, I'm here. Just that intuition I guess. Something don't feel right." He said making me feel worried all of a sudden.

"What does that mean?" I asked.

"Last time I saw Trell he was paranoid about thinking somebody was following him. I haven't heard from him since then. Let me call him or at least try to make some calls. You got that chick Liyah number? If so call her too." He gave me instructions before hanging up.

I called Liyah trying not to panic. "Sorry to wake you Liyah but have you heard from Trell?" I asked hoping she said 'yes' and not to be messy but at least to ease my damn mind.

"Hey LeLe, no I haven't spoken to Trell today at all and he didn't return none of my calls." She said. "Is he okay?" I could tell she was genuinely concerned. Poor girl really did care for Trell. It's just unfortunate that's not what his heart desired. I believe he kept her around just passing time by until him and Abbey made that final decision.

"I think he's okay. Just trying to get him on the phone that's all." I told her not wanting to alarm her. "Get some rest, didn't mean to wake you."

When I hung up I was getting ready to go hop up and go to my parents room to find out if Trell had been here. I looked out the window first and I didn't see his car. When I turned around my mother's silhouette was in my doorframe scaring the shit out of me. I hit my lamp switch turning it on. "You scared the shit out of me."

"Watch your mouth." She warned pulling her robe tighter to her body. Her hair was full of rollers and pins so she must've been to the salon earlier. "Now what's all the talk about? Where's Trell?"

"I was just about to ask you if you'd seen him any time tonight or earlier." I told her.

"I haven't seen Trell, he hasn't even called to check in today like he normally does and I figured he's been running around with one of those nappy head heffas he be running around here with."

"Him and Abbey are exclusive now ma."

"Wait, come again. Exclusive about what?"

"They're in a relationship." I told her.

She shook her head. "I don't know if that's a good or bad thing." She frowned.

"Tell me about it." I agreed.

"I'm sure Trell is fine. That boy been running the streets since a knucklehead. Get you some rest." She told me before walking away to go back in the room.

I did lay back down but that didn't mean I was going to get some rest. Not like this. I waited for Leon to call me back and it seems like it took forever. "Did you hear from him?" I asked.

"Nah, nobody ain't heard from Trell. I'm bout to get dressed and come over there. Something ain't right. I feel it." He told me before disconnecting our call. I got up and put some clothes on too feeling like I had to vomit. I called Abbey back as well.

"Nobody has heard from him. Leon is on his way over here."

"Okay, I'm on my way too then." She told me.

I hung up feeling like maybe we were overreacting cause it hadn't even been a full 24 hours yet but at the same time it was better to be safe than sorry and it wasn't like my brother to just get missing.

Chapter 14

Leandra 'LeLe' Wells

We were all gathered around the living room waiting to see if we could get Trell on the phone. It was well into the next morning so somebody should've heard something by now. We had been checking the hospitals, jails and all that and still nothing. There wasn't shit on the local news pertaining to nothing out of the ordinary so this shit was strange to me. Like, Trell wouldn't just disappear and not answer our calls. Even if he was on some bullshit somewhere with a bitch and he didn't want me to know because of Abbey, I couldn't see him not answering the phone for Leon. He had no reason to dodge his calls.

My poor mama had done smoked damn near an entire pack of cigarettes and George told her off every single time she lit one. She didn't give a fuck. That was the only thing easing her mind right now. I couldn't imagine what it felt like to be a worried mother. I tried my best to understand. I got a call from Trey and stepped outside to answer it. "Hey Trey." I spoke sounding defeated.

"Good morning shorty. Why you sound so blue? Wussup?"

"We haven't heard from Trell and that's not like him so we're just waiting around to try to see what's going on."

"How long he been missing?" He asked.

"Apparently since yesterday morning."

"Oh." He said not sounding too worried. "He's a street nigga. He could be doing anything. Trell don't sit still so give it some time."

"Leon thinks something is wrong. He keeps saying he don't feel right. That twin's intuition shit I guess."

"I mean, I'm not a twin so ion know ma. Is it anybody who got insides with any one of ya'll? When shit like this happens you gotta go back to square one. Think about it ma."

Silence.

"You there?" He asked.

"Yeah, I told him. Umm let me call you back." I told him. I didn't even wait for Trey to respond. I just hung up on him. I would have to explain later on cause right now I just didn't have the time. This was some straight up bullshit but I had a gut feeling. What he said made total sense and it didn't take me long to just think.

I rushed in the house and grabbed my keys and then slipped on some shoes before rushing out while everybody was wondering where the hell I was going. I didn't have time to talk to anybody and I knew they would be calling me so I turned my phone off. When I got to my destination, I took a deep breath and got out. I felt like my arms were heavy as hell when I knocked on the door. When it opened I was standing face-to-face with Ms. Jones. It had been years since I'd seen her face and she looked much different like the toll of the world was on her heart. She even had gray hairs now and she was still fairly young. "You've got some nerve showing up here after all this time." She gave me an evil glare. "You're not even worth me inviting you in here." She told me. Instead she came out on the porch. "Have a seat." She said to me as she sat in one of her porch chairs.

I slowly sat down and sighed. "Ms. Jones I knew I should've been came to see you. I swear I wanted to. It's just, after sending you all those letters in prison and getting no reply I knew you didn't wanna talk to me and I don't blame you."

"I sure in the hell didn't and still don't wanna talk to you now. You couldn't even imagine my pain." She said like a evil old witch. The way she glared at me with her mouth twisted up had me flabbergasted. I knew she hated me, I just didn't know it was this bad. "Why are you here now?"

"I'm here now cause I need to be. I should've been did this. I want you to know from the bottom of my heart I'm really sorry about what happened to Malik. I didn't just lose my best friend. I lost my unborn child as well. Whether you know it or not I'm still hurting but things are different now Ms. Jones. You'll soon find out the truth. What happened that night wasn't really because I was being careless. It happened because our drinks were spiked. A very jealous person from our past didn't want to see us together and because of that we both suffered a big loss."

I could tell in her eyes she probably didn't believe anything that I was saying. "How coward is that to come over here and place the blame on somebody else. Do you know what my son and me have been through?"

"I can only imagine Ms. Jones but at the same time, I lost as well. I did time in prison for something I technically didn't do. I'm still trying to build my life back.

This is killing me every single day. Sometimes I can't even sleep. If you don't believe me I can promise you that you'll find out the truth soon enough. I promise you." I explained as my lips quivered. She'd turned so cold over the years. She was never like this before.

"Why are you here?" She asked again ready to get me out of her presence.

"I... I... um." I stuttered. "My brother is missing and I just want to know have you heard from Majestic. I'm not accusing him of anything or nothing like that but I know Majestic hates me. I don't mean to be rude or nothing but I just feel like maybe he has something to do with this cause he wants to get back at me. It isn't like Trell to disappear."

She just stood up and looked at me shaking her head. She pulled her cell phone from her coat pocket and dialed a number. "She's here." She told he person on the other end confusing the shit out of me. She then passed me the phone.

I was so fucking confused I didn't know what to say or do. "I'm not touching that phone." I told her. "Put it on speaker."

She did with no problem. "Hello?" I said.

Majestic's voice boomed from the other end. "I knew yo ass was gone show up cause you to fuckin' predictable. You should've known this day was comin' LeLe. You ain't even have enough respect to come holla at me and my mama with an apology. Now, you killed my brother maybe I should kill yours." He said sending chills down my spine. I wanted to cry so bad but I wouldn't dare give neither one of them the pleasure.

"Majestic." I sighed. "Whatever you have planned please don't do this. I didn't do what you think I did. It was Kim who was behind this entire situation. She caused this, she spiked our drinks."

"I don't believe none of that shit. If she did let her tell me that."

"I don't know where she is." I told him trying to control my breathing.

"Well find her ass. You got 24 hours." He hung up.

I knew this was one of those situations where I couldn't even get the laws involved. I didn't even wanna get nobody else involved either for that matter. I didn't wanna risk anybody getting hurt or locked up. This was my problem so I had to fix it. I gave Ms. Jones one mean ass look right back cause now the fucking gloves were off.

She waited until she was back in her house hiding behind the bar door. "Hey, that's how life goes. I loss my kid, let's see how your mama feels if she loses hers. A kid for a kid." She said slamming the door missing my fucking spit by a half of second. She had me so tight I wanted to whoop that old bitch's ass. I understood she was hurt but fuck her. They were taking this shit too far.

I got in my car and sped down the street thinking about where Majestic could've taken Trell to. I told Trell not to trust that nigga. I never trusted him around my brother's cause I could see the jealousy in his eyes. I could see right past him trying to act like everything was all good.

I beat he shit out of my steering wheel as I sat at the red light crying out of anger. "Fuck! Fuck! Fuck!" I yelled aloud powering my phone back on. As soon as I did Taco Bell was calling and I didn't even answer. They were probably wondering why I hadn't showed up yet. I needed my job but right now… fuck those tacos!"

I called Karter and hopped that she picked up the phone. "Hello Queen. Today is a beautiful day to celebrate a black Princess." She cooed all cheery.

"Karter, fuck all that. I need Kim's new number and I need it now! Don't tell me you don't have it cause this is life or death. It's serious!"

"Oh um… in that case let me just call her and tell her to call you okay? I don't want to be involved in this. Five minutes okay? Five minutes." She hung up.

In exactly six minutes later my phone was ringing from an unknown number. I picked up knowing who it was.

Chapter 15

Kimberly 'Kim' Laws

I could tell from the moment I got on the phone with LeLe just how serious this was. I knew this was coming one day but I wasn't prepared. I was finally feeling at peace and enjoying my baby. I named him Majestic after his dad but gave him my last name. Majestic Jr. was the spitting image of his dad. Hell, we didn't even need a DNA to prove that. The tears rolled down my eyes as I hurried to put me and the baby a bag together. It had been seven weeks since I delivered and my baby only had to stay in the hospital two of those weeks. He was so strong and had been such a fighter. I couldn't leave him behind cause I didn't trust anyone to keep him and at the same time. This was the time for Majestic to know he had a son.

I couldn't live with him even killing off Trell cause he didn't deserve that. Nobody deserved that cause this was all on me. When I packed the bags and knew that I had Enfamil and everything for the baby, I packed up the car and then ran back inside for a few more things before locking up. I looked slightly different than the last time they'd seen me. I no longer had the fit body. Instead, I had the 'mommy' body and had gotten thick in all the right places. I chopped all of my long hair off as well and was wearing a short cut now. I just felt like it was appropriate since I was trying to turn over a new leaf but just like the devil and just like Karma. They always showed up and when we least expected it.

I had to make sure my baby was fed and feeling good and comfortable before I hit the ro. ad. Me on the other hand I couldn't even eat at all. My stomach was in knots, and fresh tears blurred my vision. I wasn't the same person they knew before I left Miami. I had learned so much about myself and come to certain terms with a lot of things about my life. I took my baby with me to church every Sunday and took an hour out of my day to read the bible every Wednesday night. if I had to leave this world I didn't wanna leave with all these demons.

I looked back at my sleeping baby. He'd brought so much joy to my life in such a little period of time. I didn't think it was possible to love somebody this much but here I was doing it and doing all by myself too. Emily and Karter helped out from time-to-time but for the most part they gave me my space so I could figure this mommy thing out my own way. Karter had told me that our mama called her asking about my son but I told her she better not tell that bitch nothing else about me, shit, tell her I disappeared. I didn't care what she told her to be honest. I just wanted her to stay far away from me.

I was making sure I went speed limit while driving cause I never wanted to drive to fast with the baby in the car and I needed some time to just think. I thought about everything I could possibly do. Emily called me multiple times and I didn't answer until I was halfway to Miami. I ignored her mostly because I knew she would try to talk me out of going or she would've at least tried to make me leave my baby with Karter and her nanny and I wasn't doing that. I needed Majestic to look in this child's eyes.

"Hello?" I finally answered with my voice cracking.

"Hey, I'm here at your apartment to drop some things off for the baby. Where are you guys?" She asked. "Are you crying?"

Silence.

"Kim, where are you?" She asked again.

I took a deep breath and told her the truth. "I'm headed home... back to Miami."

"Wait!" She yelled. "Kim..."

I cut her off and hung up powering my phone off. My mind couldn't be changed. This is what I had to do and if I had to die in the process then so be it. Sometimes this is just how the tables turned. Fuck it. "See you soon Miami." I whispered to myself. *See you real soon.*

<u>To Be Continued......</u>

CPSIA information can be obtained
at www.ICGtesting.com
Printed in the USA
LVHW081746280220
648532LV00010B/732